CW00400821

THE AXIOM FEW

Huw Langridge

Copyright © 2010 Huw Langridge

Cover illustration by Michael Langridge
Book design by Huw Langridge

All rights reserved. No part of this book may be reproduced in any form or by any electronic or mechanical means including information storage and retrieval systems, without permission in writing from the author. The only exception is by a reviewer, who may quote short excerpts in a review.

CONTENTS

INTRODUCTION

by Rod MacDonald

My first encounter with The Axiom Few was in Jupiter, the science fiction magazine. Having read fiction of all sorts since I was a boy in the 60s, it was going to take something out of the ordinary to make me sit up and take notice but I was immediately impressed by the very good characterisation and visualisation, I knew this was different and unusual. Not only was Axiom superb writing, the electric pace and the intriguing plots made this compulsive reading.

Set half a century in the future, a small group of gifted individuals fight to save not just the planet but time and space itself. Archer, Davey and Geek work in a shack beneath a motorway. Rather spartan and reclusive, they aren't in it for personal glory or even money. Few people in Britain or the planet Earth are aware that the Axiom Few have saved their hides on many occasions but that's the way they like it. They don't belong to corporations, military organisations or any other regimented outfit. They are their own people!

When reading the stories a certain word came to mind and that was... angst. A picture came to mind as well and that was The Scream by Munch. The Axiom Few exist in their own sphere of normality but outside this dimensions are being ripped apart, aliens are invading and personal lives are disappearing. The image of one of the characters swimming out into the sea on a one-way journey into the infinite oblivion is haunting in the extreme. However, there are moments of humour and the science is mind-bending in the extreme to make this overall a piece of well-balanced fiction.

In this series of eight stories, which are not isolated but connected, we are taken to exploding planets in the solar system, paradoxes in time and strange extraterrestrial artifacts. These dilemmas are in the domain of these extraordinary people but despite them being exceptionally intelligent, they are like us and it's quite easy to identify with them. When reading the stories we quickly become assimilated and their problems become our problems. That's the key to the success of the Axiom Few!

Enough of me! It's now time to get reading. I don't really have to say a great deal about this series of stories because the fiction speaks for itself. It's page turning stuff. Whatever you think I can guarantee that you won't be disappointed.

Rod Macdonald
SFCrowsnest.com

THE CERES CONFIGURATION

First published April 2004,
Jupiter SF Magazine

L ondon 2055, and the rain-lashed streets rippled and reflected the neon nightlife of this diverse city. All along the glimmering walkways of Theatreland people huddled in shop doorways escaping the dirty backwash from cars and the downpour from the grey oppressive sky.

Hunched against the rain, Archer blended into the crowd perfectly. He wore a black leather jacket and blue jeans. On the back of his jacket was the stark functional emblem of his small team of freelance techno-graduates, the Axiom Few. Below the logo was his name.

Not many people knew how important Archer was. Not many people knew that he might be the only man who could save them. Even fewer knew what he was going to save them from, and it was probably better that it stayed that way. In fact, right up until he walked into the huge reception area of the Iceberg Building, even he didn't know why he had been summoned here.

In the building, Goddard was waiting for him. This older man had lost most of his hair, and his angular nose and thin mouth gave him a stern quality that Archer had always disliked. But Goddard's eyes tried to be friendly, his handshake was bold and his voice sincere. He hobbled on a gnarled wooden cane.

'Thank you for agreeing to see me at such short notice, Archer. I realise this must be difficult for you.'

The two men entered a nearby lift and ascended to the twentieth floor, a mere quarter of the way up the towering skyscraper. They went into Goddard's office. Outside the huge window behind the old man's desk, the colourful cityscape buzzed and shimmered in the rain-mist that rose from the streets. It was a Saturday night, and Archer could think of a hundred places he would rather be.

'Please sit Archer. Now tell me, how was your trip back from La Luna?'

'It was tiring. I can never sleep on those shuttles. I could really do with some rest, and your unnecessary small-talk is keeping me from it.'

Goddard smiled and lowered himself awkwardly into his chair. He leaned his cane against the desk and crossed his palms in front of him, 'Then I'll cut straight to the chase, shall I?'

Archer nodded, and Goddard seemed to momentarily hunt for a place to begin, 'Do you know what the Ceres Belt is?'

Archer leaned back in his chair and clasped his hands behind his head, 'Yes, it's the asteroid belt that orbits the sun between Mars and Jupiter.'

'Correct. And did you know that the Space Foundation has commissioned a project to catalogue all forty thousand asteroids in the belt?'

Archer was surprised, 'Didn't they do that fifty years ago, to see if any asteroids might hit Earth?'

Goddard raised a finger, 'Ah yes, but this project serves a different purpose. You see, those asteroids were once part of a planet that exploded. This mapping project will enable us to build a computer-generated image of what the planet once looked like. The benefits to the scientific community will be far-reaching.'

Archer felt his interest growing, 'A cosmic jigsaw puzzle.'

We've got fifty ships on the project. Admittedly it's taking a lot longer than we thought. But the team are getting paid per asteroid, so we're well within budget.'

'I'm glad to hear it.' Archer didn't give a damn about the budget, 'When will the project be finished?'

Goddard tilted his head forward and looked down at his fidgeting hands, 'It's hard to say. You see, there's been a complication.'

The mining ship Khartoum established a geo-synchronous orbit over the asteroid. The spotlight's beam, which shone down from the underside of the ship's hull, illuminated the location where touchdown would take place.

A web of reinforced nylon tethers shot away from the ship, twisting and spiralling downwards under the force of their ejection. Within moments they impacted with the rock, clamping onto the dusty surface, getting a purchase as soon as they could, and kicking up plumes of age-old silicate dust as they did so.

The Khartoum swung about the stone like a child that had jumped onto a playground roundabout. The asteroid's momentum pulled the tethers tight, dragging the Khartoum along as it continued its perpetual rotation.

Once the mining ship's direction had been forcefully changed, it began to reel in the tethers on its powerful winch, bringing it closer to the surface of the asteroid. Within an hour, it had landed, and it began to drill.

Goddard picked up a remote control off his desk, 'Two months ago our seismic mapping team found an object buried three hundred metres into asteroid Euclides.

'What kind of object?'

Goddard pointed the remote control at a screen located on the wall behind Archer. Archer craned his neck around, realised he was uncomfortable, and then turned his chair to face the screen.

A picture appeared, a close up of a green circular disk mottled with tiny pinpoints that were etched into the surface. In the centre of the disk was what looked like a tiny circuit board. Alongside the object was a ruler, indicating that the whole thing was a little less than seven centimetres in diameter.

Archer felt his heart rate quicken. He turned his gaze back to Goddard, 'Does anyone know what it is?'

'We've had a lot of people working on the problem, and we have a few answers. See those markings on the surface?'

'The pinpoints?'

'Yes. Well, we counted them. There are over forty thousand of the blighters.' Goddard pointed at the screen, 'The quality of this picture doesn't do it justice. But if you look closely at the actual artifact, the level of detail and craftsmanship is quite amazing.'

'Forty thousand,' said Archer in a soft voice, 'One for every...'

'...asteroid in the belt.' Goddard finished. 'We've been able to work out that much. And we've had some clever people doing some serious number-crunching, trying to work out exactly what it all means.'

'Have you drawn any conclusions?'

'Yes, but we may be too late. You see; the pinpoints on the artifact are a depiction of the layout of the asteroids at a particular point in time; a configuration that has not yet been reached.'

'How long until it is reached?'

'A few hours. We can't be absolutely sure however. Calculating the trajectories of forty thousand asteroids isn't easy, as you may well imagine. Especially when you need to add in the gravitational perturbations that they inflict on each other. The necessary calculations are astronomical, in every sense of the word.'

Archer stood and walked over to the window. Suddenly the city looked like a different place; an alien place. How did an object like that find its way into an asteroid? Was this the final incontrovertible evidence of the existence of alien intelligence? And more importantly...

'What will happen when the configuration is reached?' he asked Goddard.

Goddard sighed, took his cane and struggled to his feet before moving towards the door. 'We don't know for certain. But we think we have a pretty good idea. Now, will you follow me? There's something I want to show you.'

The swishing sound of the rain and the rushing sound of the cars merged into one under the motorway bridge where the Axiom Few test shack had been erected.

A tall man carrying a leather jacket which he used as a hood against the downpour, made his way towards the shack. Anyone standing behind him would have seen the Axiom Few emblem and the word "Davey" written across the back of his jacket. But, save for the cars, there was no one for miles, and that was exactly why they had put the shack here, hidden away from prying eyes.

Davey opened the corrugated metal door of the shack and entered. Negotiating his way around a mess of wires, tools, computers and disks, shivering and shaking rain from his hair, he made his way over to his colleague, who did not wear a leather jacket, but instead wore an Axiom Few t-shirt with the name "Geek" written below the ubiquitous logo.

Hanging on a clotheshorse in the middle of the shack, Davey noticed the shiny suit they had been working on, which looked like it was made of thousands of lenses. Leading away from the back of the helmet was a fat bunch of coloured wires which trailed across the floor and up onto the desk where Geek was sitting. He was connecting them to a computer terminal.

'Damn it's wet out there,' said Davey.

'Did anyone see you?'

'Of course not. How's the prototype coming along?'

Geek smiled. 'You're just in time for a test run. Wanna put it on?'

Archer and Goddard stepped out of the office and approached the lifts. Archer's head was buzzing, and he was full of questions about the alien artifact, but he tried to maintain an inner resolve.

'Did they find anything else during the mission?'

'No. The Foundation has mapped seventy-three per-cent of the belt now, but they've found nothing else unusual.' Goddard pressed the button on the lift.

'Where are we going?' said Archer.

The lift arrived. The doors opened.

'Archer, do you know why we call this the Iceberg Building?' They stepped into the lift.

'Because it's always so damn cold?'

Goddard pressed a button. The lift doors closed and they began to descend. Archer watched as the numbers on the lift's display started to count down from twenty to ten to one, then Ground and Lower Ground. Suddenly they had reached floor minus-one, minus-two, and the minus figures counted up as they continued to descend. The numbers counted faster as their descent speed increased. The numbers changing rapidly, climbing past fifty, then one hundred then five-hundred.

Archer felt no difference in the lift. Actually, it felt as though they weren't moving at all. Though he began to feel a little ill when the lift numbers went into four figures, he realised that his nausea was psychological, he was imagining the floors rushing by outside, and he struggled to suppress the uncomfortable sensation.

'So Archer,' said Goddard calmly. 'How long have you been with the Axiom Few?'

Archer ignored him. Goddard didn't take the hint. 'Are you glad they pulled you out of the sea?'

Archer tried his best not to let a response register on his face. He stared at the rapidly changing floor numbers.

'Why did you jump Archer? Was it something to do with the scar on your face?'

Archer uttered a low grunt. 'You gave me that scar Dad. And yes, if you really want to know. That's exactly why I jumped.'

The lift stopped at floor minus 3472. There was an understated ping as the lift doors opened.

Goddard placed a hand on Archer's shoulders. 'We have an important task to work on. It's vital that we forget our differences for now.'

'Believe me. The only reason I came was because the Space Foundation promised to fund the Axiom Few's ventures for another six months. I'm not here to do you any favours.' Goddard nodded, and shifted his gaze toward the door. 'As long as we know where we stand. Please follow me.'

Archer followed Goddard out into a cold underground corridor, where muddy water cascaded down the walls and his breath was visible in front of his face. Harsh bright lights ran in a strip along the length of the tunnel, which stretched for about fifty metres downhill away from them and then snaked around a corner. Round that very corner came a young woman dressed in a white lab coat that was several sizes too big for her.

Goddard leaned towards Archer, and Archer caught an unpleasant whiff of whisky on his breath when he spoke. His voice gated by the cylindrical tunnel. 'We're nine kilometres down into the crust now.' He turned to the woman, 'Good evening Rachel.'

Rachel smiled. She was holding three pairs of goggles, and she handed one to Archer, then Goddard, before putting the third pair on herself.

Goddard put his on, and Archer followed. Archer was apprehensive, and hated Goddard more with every passing minute. Hated him from bringing up the past. Why couldn't they have just kept things professional?

They began to make their way along the tunnel, Rachel in front, followed by Goddard, who turned occasionally to continue his disclosure to Archer.

'When the oil companies came to shoot seismic over this whole area, they didn't find any hydrocarbons - at least, none of a commercial quantity. But what they did find scared the living daylights out of them. So they alerted the authorities, who in turn alerted the Space Foundation. What they found was…'

'They found another artifact, right?' Archer interrupted, unsure of whether to smile or frown. Somehow he managed both.

'Precisely. But things are a bit different with this one. It's light and motion sensitive. It actually fires some kind of lightning bolt at anyone or anything that tries to approach it. So far it's killed twelve people. Twelve people! The one up at Euclides didn't defend itself like this one does.'

They stopped outside a hatchway set into the wall. Rachel opened it and walked in, Goddard and Archer followed. They were in a tiny room, barely larger than the lift. Archer became increasingly apprehensive when Rachel closed the hatch behind them and flicked a switch, plunging the room into absolute darkness. A moment later Archer could see. Everything was red, and he understood the nature of the goggles.

In the grainy infrared enhanced gloom Rachel turned to the opposite wall and opened another hatchway. They followed her into little cavern with a low ceiling, which actually turned out to be a small upper ledge near the roof of a much larger cavern, which stretched out below them.

Goddard pointed down towards the centre of the cavern, 'Can you see it?'

Archer looked down, and could just make out a small stone plinth at the base of the cavern, about a hundred metres away. On top of the plinth sat another artifact, embedded in the rock.

'But surely, if we can see it, then it can see us, right?'

'Wrong. It's proximity based. From this distance we're okay, but go anywhere closer...'

Archer's eyes tried to make out the other features in the cave, but found he was struggling to see anything but rock, 'So this one's protecting itself.'

Rachel spoke, 'Yes. We think that's because it hasn't been triggered yet.'

'Triggered?'

Goddard stepped right in front of Archer blocking his view of the artifact, 'Think about it. There we were, trying to recreate a virtual reality image of the planet that once exploded and eventually became the Ceres Asteroid Belt. We were hoping to find out what caused the explosion in the first place. But then we found the smoking gun, buried inside Euclides.

'You see Archer, it's a chain reaction.'

'A domino effect across the solar system, and... and the layout depicted on the artifact is the timed-trigger for the next explosion.'

'Precisely,' replied Goddard.

Archer shook his head in disbelief, 'What kind of civilisation would rig up a complex set of time bombs like this?'

Goddard waved a finger in front of Archer's face, he was smiling, but it was a sinister smile, 'A profound question Archer. I have my theories. We may have finally spotted them watching us from the sun. But I'm afraid it is a conundrum for another day. Right now our priority is to disarm the thing.'

'Wait, wait, disarm it? You've been able to build around it so far. How did you build this cavern?'

'It was already here.'

'But – the hatchway, the tunnels.'

'Machines built those.'

'Well can't you get machines to help you now?'

'Too clumsy, and we don't understand the technology. We need a human to do the job. Now, if you could somehow use that light distortion jacket your mob have invented, maybe we could...'

Archer interrupted. 'Why didn't you tell me this when I was on La Luna? I could have easily requested to return to Earth earlier.'

'It was only a couple of days ago that all this fell into place for us. What I have told you today is the culmination of months of hard detective work.'

'Why can't we hurl the thing into space?'

'We already tried to move it. We tried to cut it out of the rock. I lost a very good friend that day. Now, will you bring the suit?'

In the Axiom Few test shack Davey gazed apprehensively down at the suit he was now wearing. To Geek, Davey seemed to be in awe of it. Perhaps that was not a good thing, for Geek knew that technology was not to be feared.

'Okay,' said Geek, 'don't move. I'm increasing the light distortion ratio.'

He started to tap commands into his computer. Within a few

moments Geek thought he saw the corrugated metal wall of the shack directly behind Davey. Davey was looking down at himself.

'My God,' he said. 'It's working.'

'Hold still. Just a little longer. Do you feel nauseous at all? The electromagnetic field can have that effect.'

'No, no I feel fine. This is amazing!'

'Congratulations Davey, you're about to be the world's first invisible man.'

Archer, Goddard and Rachel stepped out of the dark hatchway into the light of the tunnel that led up to the lifts.

'You haven't left me with much time,' Archer said, 'the suit is miles away from here. Just a few hours until the configuration is reached you say?'

'Give or take a few days.'

'That's not funny. I could get one of the other members of my team to bring it down, but they wouldn't get here for hours. Who knows how long it would take to get an idea of the workings of that bomb.'

Goddard's face began to wrinkle into an expression of pleading, 'It's our only hope Archer. We have no other technology that is up to the task. You don't realise how ahead of the game your little team is. The real innovation doesn't germinate in the large corporations. It's the little guys like you who do the pioneering stuff. That's why the Foundation wants to sponsor you. We haven't the time to deal with red tape. We need to start working right away.'

Archer nodded, 'It's funny to see you finally needing me after all these years. I bet you never thought you'd see the day when you had to beg me to help you. You are begging, aren't you?'

'Don't be a stupid fool. You're not doing me any favours. You're doing your species a favour. This is bigger than both of us.'

'You're right of course,' replied Archer, feeling a sense of quiet justice that he was in a position of power over his father for once,

'Then I suppose I'd better start making arrangements. Maybe I can get close enough to that thing to...' his voice trailed off as he heard distant running footsteps, and realised that someone was coming down the corridor towards them. A man in a loose blue shirt with rolled up sleeves and beige docker pants rounded the corner and bounded up to Goddard, sweat stained and out of breath.

'Goddard, sir. Sorry to disturb you, but we've had a number of reports from the Mars Orbiter crew. They've been getting some strange electrical and magnetic disturbances from the surface. They don't know what to make of it. They're streaming the data back now.'

Goddard's eyes quickly met Archers, 'Mars!' he whispered sharply. 'Of course! Mars is between the asteroid belt and Earth. It's Mars next.'

'There's your bloody domino effect,' whispered Archer.

Against the scarred, reddish-orange backdrop of the planet's surface, the Mars Orbiter ship cruised along its orbital path.

The apparent calmness and serenity outside the small craft was juxtaposed by the frantic voices within.

'The radiation levels have trebled in the last twenty minutes. The nephelometer reports a massive increase in particle density in the atmosphere. It's like the whole planet is shaking itself apart. Maybe the Foundation can make something of it, because I sure as hell can't.'

There was an almighty rumble that shook the Orbiter. Peering through the view-port one of the astronauts could see the northern hemisphere of the planet looming above them. Fissures began to appear in the rock. The planet began to dissolve in slow motion as explosions ruptured and distorted the Valles Marineris, the high cliffs collapsing into the huge rift. And Olympus Mons, the seventy-kilometre wide mountain, was sliding apart like it was nothing more than a child's sandcastle.

A huge chunk of rock, tossed away from the planet by the huge blast was heading straight for the Orbiter.

They fired the thrusters to alter their trajectory, but the piece of the planet was too large to escape. It grew larger in the viewport, obscuring the remnants of the doomed world below. The crew of the Orbiter, and the ground staff at the Foundation all knew that it was impossible to be that close to an exploding planet and survive.

'Davey,' said Geek, 'where are you, man? I can't see you. Did you move?'

'No, I didn't move. I stayed right where I was. Isn't this just the best!'

'Fantastic! I knew I needed to polarize the upper-spectrum four times instead of three. There's always some little technicality that just...'

The lights dimmed slightly. Geek said, 'I think the generator's failing.'

'Should we stop the test? Something like that might...'

The lights went out. In the complete darkness the two men fell silent, all that could be heard was their breathing, and the stuttering of the electrical generator winding down outside the shack. Then a moment later the lights came on full. Bulbs began to pop and computer terminals blew. Davey faded back to visibility; the lenses in the suit lighting up like a Christmas tree. As he looked down at himself, small ripples of blue electric light began to course up and down the length of the suit.

Davey looked at Geek, 'Is this meant to happen?'

Geek became frantic, 'Get it off. It doesn't have a surge suppressant yet. It's going to explode. Get out of it now!'

'What the hell would cause a surge?' They both began to fumble with the suit, hurriedly pulling it off Davey. It was hot to the touch, and Geek knew that an explosion was imminent.

Once Davey was out of the suit, the two men threw it across

the shack. It landed in the corner, a trail of wires scraping along the floor behind it. The suit popped and fizzed, then exploded in a blinding flash of blue light as it impacted with the side of the shack. Flames began to lick up the wall. Geek reached for a fire extinguisher, and doused the flames. Seconds later, the suit was nothing more than a smouldering pile of charred electronics.

There was a moment of disbelieving silence between the two men, punctuated by the rattle of rain on the tin roof, and an awful smell of burnt plastic.

Geek's mobile phone began to ring.

They had returned to Goddard's office. The old man was pacing back and forth near the window, one hand stroking his balding head, the other grasping his cane. Archer stared out at the dark city.

'We've been hit with the electromagnetic effects. Surely there are gravitational implications for every planet in the solar system when one of its bodies is destroyed.'

There was a knock on the door and the scientist entered without waiting for permission.

'Sir,' he said resignedly, 'we've lost the Orbiter.' Goddard stopped pacing, but remained silent.

Archer spoke, 'Mars was next in line. The Earth artifact is still armed. It's protecting itself because it hasn't delivered its payload yet. There's going to be another artifact hidden somewhere in the new Martian asteroids. We need to find it, just like we did with Ceres, because without it we can't calculate when Earth's time is up.'

Goddard stared at Archer, 'Then you must get the suit. Quickly.'

Archer left the Iceberg Building and tipped his head up to the sky, feeling the cool rain on his cheeks. He pulled his mobile phone from his jacket, he dialled Geek's mobile.

When the call was answered, Archer said, 'It's me. I need you to prep the LDJ.'

'What the hell for?' said Geek at the other end.

'Because tomorrow I have to save the world.'

There was a long pause on the line, 'Geek, are you still there?'

'Yes I'm here. Listen, can't you do it next week?'

There was a beep on the line. Archer said, 'Hold on Geek I've got another call coming through.'

Archer switched to the other call, 'Archer speaking.'

'It's your father. I've just had a call from our office in Cape Town. Listen. There's a diamond mine down there, near Pretoria. The Cullinan Diamond Mine. It's the deepest shaft in the world. Two deaths were reported yesterday at the rock face.'

'What's that got to do with anything? Listen. I was thinking. Maybe we're being taught a lesson here; a lesson about the destructive nature of man. Perhaps our race is finally getting a taste of its own medicine.'

'Archer, listen to what I'm telling you, dammit! Save the speculation for later. Right now we have a bigger problem. They've found another artifact in South Africa. Don't you see what that means?'

'What?'

'It means no matter what we do, Archer. Even if we are successful in using your suit to disarm this bomb, the damn things are buried in the rock. They could be anywhere and we don't know how many there are. So, how will we really know if we got them all?'

THE DARKEN LOOP

First published January 2009,
Jupiter SF Magazine

S he would see all of today, but she wouldn't know why.

It was a sunny spring morning in London in early May 2052, and the young woman stepped off the train and made her way towards the teeming Waterloo concourse. She hated this time of the morning, when thousands of fellow passengers navigated their way through to the exits and off to start another day at the office. She herself was heading for a job interview as a researcher at the computer labs at Kings College London. Whether she would get the job, she had no real idea. This was her second interview and she was under no illusion that she could be up against a good many candidates that may be more qualified for the position than she.

She needed a coffee. Perhaps a cappuccino would help her sharpen some blunt edges, make her perform better. She felt into her bag for the free coffee voucher she'd put in there that morning. Luckily she had spotted it on the bedroom floor the night before. The voucher expired today.

◆ ◆ ◆

GEEK?

Geek clutched his head and looked across the kitchen at Davey, who was spooning sugar into his mug of tea. 'Who's that?'

Davey turned, startled. 'Who's who?'

Don't worry about that for now. I want you to do as I say.

Geek saw that it wasn't Davey who spoke at all. 'Sorry, I thought I heard a voice.'

You did hear a voice, but I don't want your friend to think you've gone insane, so for now I just want you to listen.

'Davey there's a voice in my head. I think I might have gone insane.'

'Hah, I knew it. But is there *method* to your madness?'

'Just let me talk to the voice for a sec, okay. I promise I've not gone mad. I think.'

Davey held his hands up. 'Whatever you say.'

There was something about being a member of the Axiom Few, this small band of freelance techno-graduates, that meant that you could command a level of unquestionable understanding from the other guys in the team. Corporations so wrapped up in their own bureaucracy would approach the Few to develop ideas without having to navigate their own red tape and hierarchical sign-offs. A rogue bunch like the Axiom Few could get to work on an idea and usually yield results in a fraction of the time. Their power of invention was leading edge, raw, and often downright terrifying. But it required trust. 'Okay, voice in my head' said Geek. 'I'm all yours.'

I knew I'd picked the right man. Somehow I don't think others would have been so easily convinced.

'You're still on borrowed time, my friend. What's your transmission device?' asked the Geek.

Never mind about that. There's something I need you to do.

'You have to tell me who you are first.'

If I did you wouldn't believe me.

Davey carried the two mugs over to the kitchen table and sat down opposite Geek. Geek took a sip of his sugary tea. 'I have a very good imagination.'

Did you ever imagine then, that by the time a computer was powerful enough to pass a Turing test, it might also be capable of communicating directly with a human brain without interface?

'I can't say it ever crossed my mind.'

Davey said, 'What's he saying?'

Geek raised his hand to silence Davey, waiting for the voice to continue. 'He's a she.'

Davey raised his eyebrows and nodded encouragingly, 'Stop the press. Geek's finally pulled a chick.'

'Prove that you are what you say you are,' said Geek.

Why don't you prove that I'm not?

Geek contemplated this for a moment. Then he looked squarely at Davey. 'Call Archer. I think we're in trouble.' No questions. Davey reached for his mobile.

Geek said, 'Computers aren't powerful enough to pass a Turing test. They never quite nail it. It'll be years. I've tried programming...'

What makes you think that I'm even in your timeline?

'Now you're talking rubbish,' but Geek didn't really believe himself on that one.

Davey's mobile had connected to Archer. He spoke into the receiver.

Archer was holding the phone when it buzzed in his hand, taking him by surprise. Pitching his half-smoked cigarette in the direction of the setting sun, he stepped into the relative silence of the Axiom Few test shack, which stood hidden away beneath a motorway overpass 40 miles outside London. Once inside, the drone of rush hour cars was muffled but constant.

He put the phone to his ear and said 'Hello?'

'Archer, can you get to Geek's apartment?'

'Davey, I'm...'

'This is urgent. Geek's asking for you.' No more questions.

Davey was the moneyman of the Few; and often the conscience of the team. Accountants could sometimes get under your skin, but behind all the spreadsheets was Geek's best and oldest friend. A man without whom Geek was prepared to forgo joining the Few in the first place. That was loyalty. But Archer wasn't an enemy of Davey. They saw eye to eye now, a lot more than they had in the past. Back when there was all that stuff about... her.

About Louise.

Geek himself was the undoubtedly the brains of the Few, but he needed leadership, and that was where Archer provided direction and support. Geek's inventions had enabled Archer's team to finance their lives and operations for the last seven years. They needed him, and they happily indulged his ideas and concepts.

No questions.

'I'm on my way.'

There's no need to type out our conversation, Geek. I can just as easily email you a transcript of what is said. Though you may not want me to.

Geek was sitting at the computer in his workshop. He had opened a Word document and was about to start typing.

Opening his mail client, Geek said. 'You need to convince me you're not a hoax? You can't play me for a fool. Even though you do have quite a sexy voice.'

Davey had remained in the kitchen to talk to Archer. Now Geek could hear him on the phone to Louise, telling her he was going to be home late. It sounded like she wasn't too pleased. It sounded like she was going to go over to a girlfriend's house instead of waiting in for him.

Geek saw the email in his inbox. The sender was

BRANCH8A66H088111F2@YOURDOMAIN.COM.

'Yourdomain. Very funny,' said Geek as he opened the message.

He recognised the first line of the email instantly. *GEEK?* It read just like the start of their conversation.

I had to resort to hexadecimal to rationalise the branching but it's much more quantum than that as you'd undoubtedly agree if you were to look at the permutations. I also had to truncate my username, as your mail servers wouldn't be able to handle full length of the address. And as for the domain? What idiot thought of domain structure used in the early web. Ridiculous!

'Hardly early! The web's been around for sixty years.' Geek sat back in his geeky leather computer chair. 'Now you really have to start explaining yourself.'

When your friend Davey called Archer, Archer was at your test-shack. Is that where the goggles are located? Geek sat forward, 'How did you know about the...'

About the goggles?

'The test-shack! That's a well-kept...'

Never mind about that. Just get him to bring the goggles.

Geek stood and made his way back to the kitchen. Davey said, 'Gotta go,' to his girlfriend and ended his call. 'Get back onto Archer and tell him to grab the goggles.' No questions. Davey did as Geek said.

Archer was already in his car on the motorway slip road when Davey's second call came through.

'Geek wants you to bring the goggles.'

'Ah for God's sake,' said Archer as he joined the outer lane, dropping the phone to his lap as a police car raced past. 'Ok, I'll get them. I'll be about half an hour.'

Archer reached between his legs and ended the call on the phone, then he started looking for the next turn-off.

Your branch hasn't even nailed quantum computers, let alone dabbled in the string elements. Of course it had to be a hex email address.

'What are these branches you're referring to?' Geek had grabbed a wad of A4 paper from the printer. On the top sheet he started drawing a crude picture of a tree. He was trying to understand. He was trying to be faster than her. Faster than *it*.

You're on the right track. The Multiverse theory implies that all pos-

sible universes exist, and that's true to a point. But they're not infinite. They branch. There are lots of them. Oh Geek, lots and lots and lots of them, but at the Big Bang singularity, well there was only one branch then. Or perhaps you could call it the trunk.

Geek was scratching his head. Davey laughed absurdly across the kitchen. Geek knew why. When a man with Geek's IQ started scratching his head, it was time to worry. Geek smiled at this.

You make a decision. The universe splits. You make another decision. There are always two outcomes. To do or not to do. The universe splits. We're always at the top of the tree. There are many, many branches. But we all know about fractal geometry; there's always room for another split, because it's all a matter of magnification.

Geek was nodding. 'You're on a different branch. I understand where you're coming from now. Just tell me what you want me to do. And then maybe we can negotiate.'

I need you to help Davey's girlfriend get a cup of coffee on the way to work.

'That's an interesting request. When do you want me to do it?'

Exactly one year ago tomorrow. And now I'm going to show you how.

'She's gone over to Emily's flat,' said Davey, running his hands through his straggly long blonde hair. 'She was mad at me for staying out. I think they're going to get a bottle of wine and a takeaway. What the hell does Louise have to do with all of this?'

Archer had arrived by then and all three of them stood around the kitchen table, on top of which lay the goggles he had picked up from the test-shack. Geek was connecting a laptop to the data port on the goggles.

Archer placed his hand on them. 'We haven't even tested these babies yet.' In his head, he too was wondering why his ex- and Davey's current girlfriend was being dragged into this bizarre circumstance. Archer and Davey had come to an agreement nearly four years previously that the Louise affair would not impact on the work of the Axiom Few. And yet here she was, dead centre of one of their projects, even though no one yet knew why. Except Geek, of course, who was always ahead of the curve.

Geek hadn't yet completed work on the invention of the goggles. He had told Archer only a week earlier that he was going to need another month to re-program the code that processed the reflection data. He'd had to start from scratch when he realised that the code he'd used till now was producing anomalous results; upside down images, artifacts that didn't belong in the frame.

The goggles themselves had been designed to look round corners, in a way. They would take in what light they saw, like binoculars, and build new images from the reflections in the first image. The best example of this, and the one Geek would always use when trying to explain his project, was that if you imagined a car sitting at a set of traffic lights in front of you at the end of a road on a sunny day, it's metal and glass would reflect images that you could not see directly. If you magnified part of a reflection of a curved surface you would be able to see down the road the car was turning into, out of your line of sight. These multiple images could then be snapshotted, unwarped, and viewed in slideshow through the goggles. Ideal for when the viewer wanted to see around corners.

'We may not have to test them,' said Geek. 'According to the Bitch From Another Dimension...'

He paused a moment before continuing.

'...or Brenda as she prefers to be called, the goggles work just fine as they are, for the purpose at hand. Though I'm yet to be convinced.'

After a moment Archer shrugged, agreeing in his mind to sit back and see how this whole thing might unfold, but, as leader of the team, be ready to pull the plug on this whenever it looked like it might be necessary. That this was about Louise unnerved him more than he cared to let on.

I've sent you two more emails. For now I want you to open only the first one.

Geek accessed his web-mail from the browser on the laptop. Two unread emails sat in his inbox from Brenda. He opened the first. The email was full of computer code.

Paste this code into the goggle software program just after your first image-processing sub-routine.

Geek scanned the code. Keen to see what this would do to his software, he did as Brenda instructed.

Now re-compile the code.

Geek activated the compiler, and waited for it to complete.

The two others watched in silence.

Put the goggles on.

Geek disconnected the cable from the goggles and lifted the strap over his head, reminding himself that he needed to make the whole unit a hell of a lot lighter if it was ever going to become commercial.

The world through the goggles looked just the same as without them. Archer and Davey were gawping at him in glorious technicolour. Geek reached up to the side panel that sat near his right ear to switch to one of the other, reflected, images, when Brenda stopped him.

Don't change the image. Just wait a few moments.

Geek lowered his hand, and waited.

And there it was. A sudden rent appeared in the space between where Archer and Davey stood. It was as through reality had unzipped for a moment and through the torn seam he could still see the kitchen, but the light was different and there was a young boy sitting at the kitchen table, eating a plate of chips. Within a few seconds the slice closed, returning the kitchen to normality.

'What the bloody hell was that?' yelled Geek, hauling off the goggles and throwing them onto the table.

Relax.

Archer and Davey were coming round the table to him now, both bearing looks of acute concern. 'What the bloody hell was what?' said Davey.

Things go through it. You can send things to that place. That time.
'When?'
Exactly one solar cycle. A year.
'That boy was living here then. I moved in six months ago.'
That's correct.

And now Geek understood. 'Ok Brenda,' said Geek. 'I understand the how, but I still need to understand the why. Why should we help you? What's in it for us?'

Trust me. When you know everything. Your two friends will be tripping over themselves to do this.

The second email from Brenda contained an attachment. It was a voucher for a free medium cappuccino at the Costa Coffee on the concourse at Waterloo Station. The boys stood and watched while Geek's seemingly one-sided conversation continued.

'What am I supposed to do with this?'

Rips like the one you saw appear and disappear all the time. You can't always know when and where, and as you know they don't appear for long. And you can't even see them with the naked eye. Your goggles can see them...

'That I already know.'

...so can dogs and cats. And as for where? Well, I've started to learn how to calculate the probabilities, but I haven't got there yet. So I rely on chance to some degree. It's important to note that the expiry date on the voucher is tomorrow. Tomorrow a year ago, that is.

'So what do I need to do?'

Get to Davey's apartment. I have predicted with some degree of certainty that a rip will appear for approximately fifty-five seconds inside Davey and Louise's bedroom, between the door and the bed. It will happen tonight. It is a perfect position for her to discover the voucher, if you were to drop it through the hole before it closes up.

'Okay. I think I can do that. But why?'

And whatever you do, you must not look anywhere else in the room through the rip. You must not see anything other than the floor of the

*room. Even if you see things, you must not see them. Do you under-
stand? I need you to know that Louise's life is hanging in the balance.*

'I've pondered this temporal stuff before,' said Geek. 'So I
thought it would be something like that. But I need to know why
it's so important we save her.'

*If you talk about what you see, the consequences might require that
I seed another project to remove your friend Archer from the timeline.
And I wouldn't want to do that unless it was absolutely necessary.*

Geek nodded, 'Okay.'

*Now I think you have some explaining to do. You have two hours
until the rip appears.*

And now Geek was talking about going over to Davey's flat. Archer
felt a sinking sensation deep down in his stomach. He had managed to avoid such a visit till now. He'd managed to avoid seeing
a snapshot of the life that Davey and Louise had built for themselves after she'd left him. Pictures of them together in bars and
on beaches. The smell of the Coco Mademoiselle she always wore.
A dark cloak settled over his heart.

'Geek, look. What the hell is all this about?'

'Brenda's telling me that Louise will die if we don't do this.'

'Die?' Archer's stomach tightened, and no doubt Davey's reaction was similar. This was becoming more bizarre by the
minute.

Davey hugged himself, 'Why would she die?'

Geek printed off the second email, gathering his thoughts. He
picked up the Costa Coffee voucher that expired a year ago tomorrow. 'It's like this,' Geek continued, clearly uneasy about the
fact that he was talking about a girl that was, in some way, close
to both Davey's and Archer's hearts. 'The goggles, with their new
software, are able to see... rips. Rips in time. We can send things
through these rips.' He held up the voucher. 'We need to drop this
onto the bedroom floor of your apartment Davey, tonight.'

Davey's eyebrows lifted a full inch in surprise. Archer grabbed the voucher from Geek's hand and read it. 'It's expired.'

'The rip opens to the same place one year earlier. One year ago. Which means, after we drop it though, the voucher will expire tomorrow.'

Davey started laughing in a manner that was both nervous and ridiculed. He seemed to be searching for words to rationalise what he was hearing.

Archer spared him the trouble. 'No questions Davey, remember?'

Davey settled himself and nodded. 'How's she gonna die?'

Geek was silent a moment, looking up towards the ceiling as he listened to the voice that was speaking in his head. Then he spoke.

'In the rush hour traffic on the Waterloo Road,' he said. 'She'll be accidentally shoved in front of a refrigerated food lorry. It won't be anybody's fault. She'll just get shoved by the crowd waiting to cross at the lights.'

Archer considered this for a moment and said. 'So sending her the coffee voucher must delay her in some way.'

Davey added, 'Okay, yes. So she decides to get a coffee when she wasn't going to before, and misses the lorry. She misses being shoved.'

Archer's nerves were standing on end. 'Then what the hell are we waiting for?'

They were all in Archer's car. Archer drove and Geek sat in the back seat, continuing his dialogue with Brenda. The two boys in the front seat remained silent, both no doubt thinking about Louise.

You asked me earlier why I'm doing this? Why am I going to all this effort to save Davey's girlfriend? Let me tell you. I need to exist. Without me humanity would have been extinct a long time now. Among other things, I am responsible for preventing the Voidant War in seventeen point eight trillion branches.

'I've never heard of the Voidant War.'

Archer and Geek both said, 'What?' from the front seats.

Precisely my point Geek. I have saved countless ignorant lives through my predictions of wars, natural disasters, asteroid strikes, dictatorships. Louise and Davey, they have a child together, and somewhere down the line their child grows up to patent the code that led to my creation. One of the challenges of my existence is to ensure my existence in as many branches as possible, because of all the reasons I have given. The Global Consortium, the Space Foundation and the Humanity Council have given me the license to do my work. By helping me you are not just saving Louise's life. You are saving billions of others too. You are helping to close a Darken Loop. And with every Loop I close, mankind lives a little longer. Extinction gets pushed a little further away.

'Does this Darken Loop point back to our own timeline?' said Geek.

It cannot. Paradoxes prevail, Geek. If you were changing your own past right now, then Louise would have already been dead a year. We are changing neither my branch or yours. We are changing the branches where millions have already died. We are saving those lost people so that civilization has more chances at survival further down the road.

Louise was still out at Emily's when they got to Davey's flat, which was handy under the circumstances. Geek thought that the last thing they needed was to complicate an already complicated situation with the resurrected difficulties of an old love-triangle, not to mention the questions that she would have about why the three of them were hanging out in her bedroom with what looked suspiciously like a pair of oversized x-ray specs and an expired Costa Coffee voucher.

Davey led them into the bedroom and threw some clothes off the bed so that the three of them could sit on it. Archer did not sit however, and chose to loiter near the window that looked down onto the quiet street below.

The rip is due to appear any minute near the door. You'll have to be ready for it, and when it appears, make sure you don't put any of your body through it. Keep your hands back and just push the voucher through the hole.

'I could make a paper plane and throw it through.'

No. You couldn't guarantee that she would open it up and see the voucher. She may just throw it in the bin. Just be careful. You'll have almost a minute, so there's no need to rush.

They waited a while, not speaking. An awkward atmosphere had developed, and Geek was not unwise to the cause and circumstances of the weighty silence that hung in the air between Archer and Davey. Geek was unable to think of anything to say on the matter, so he chose to stay quiet too.

Put the glasses on Geek.

Geek strapped the goggles to his head and started to look around the room. Almost immediately a rip appeared near the window where Archer was standing and Geek moved towards it.

Not that one!

The rip closed a second later.

Like I said, there's another longer one coming along near the door. It's a better position for her to find the voucher.

Geek pulled away from the space where the rip had been and smiled nervously at the others. 'False alarm. God, look at my hands shaking!'

And then the rip opened near the door. The one Brenda had expected. Geek moved towards it, bending slightly.

Careful now. Don't be hasty.

Geek approached the fissure, and for a moment he tried to memorise the image of its sides. They seemed to glow slightly as though, where the fabric of time had been opened, there was a fire of burning chemicals and particles that were forcing the rip to be held in its open state. They seemed to shimmer and fold. The other two stepped closer to where he was, but he ignored them.

Drop it now.

Geek pushed the voucher through the rip, taking care to pull his hand back before it got too near to the hole. The paper slid through and floated on the air for a moment before flipping over on its way to the floor. For a moment it looked like it was going to land face down, but it flipped again, and landed on the blue carpet of that year-old bedroom.

'Wow, did you see it disappear? Just like that!' said Davey, his voice full of childish wonder.

'Amazing,' said Archer, who had now bent forward to where Geek was.

Both had clearly forgotten about their earlier tension, and were now in awe of what, to them, was a disappearing piece of paper.

Geek had a different view as his goggles showed him the different branch. And just before the rip closed up forever, leaving the voucher on the other side of it, he caught a reflection in the mirror.

'My God!'

The words escaped his mouth before he'd had a chance to stop them. He stood up fully and clicked the side of the goggles to access the image he thought he had seen. The image switched to that reflection, and he confirmed it to be true. Davey had been lying in the bed with a woman. A woman who was clearly *not* Louise. He tried to stifle his reaction, but it was too late. Of course, Davey already might know what Geek had seen (would he have already given any thought to what he was up to in this room a year before), but Archer wouldn't know. Archer didn't know, and it had to stay that way.

'What did you see?' said Archer.

Geek shook his head. 'Nothing. It was nothing.'

'Tell us, Geek. What did you see?' He swiped the goggles from Geek's head and put them on.

'Archer, no.'

But it was too late. Archer was already seeing the image and his mouth dropped open. 'You were cheating on her. Davey, you complete bastard.'

Davey was clearly still trying to piece it all together. 'What are you talking about?'

But Archer continued, tearing off the goggles and throwing them at Davey. They bounced off his chest and fell to the floor. 'You stole her from me and then you cheated on her. You don't bloody deserve her. You're a disgrace.' Geek spoke up. 'Archer you need to forget...' 'Now listen here,' Davey said.

'Just you try and deny it. Are you trying to deny it?'

After a moment, Davey lowered his head and shook it. 'No.'

'Does she know?'

Davey looked resigned, but almost pleading, 'Of course not.'

And now Archer's finger was pointing at Davey's chest, jabbing the other man accusingly. 'Then you better tell her.' Davey said nothing, but met Archer's eyes squarely, defiantly.

'Tell her Davey, or I'll tell her for you.' Archer made his way to the door. To Geek he said, 'I assume we're done here now? I can go? Did we save her?'

Geek waited for a response from Brenda, but no voice spoke, making him wonder what the consequences of their actions had really been. He nodded anyway, and gave Archer the answer he wanted to hear. 'Yes, we saved her.'

But what he didn't say was that, despite their actions, maybe they hadn't saved Archer.

They all heard the key in the front door at the other end of the apartment.

Louise was back.

Archer drove home struggling to push dark tears to the back of his eyes and a jealous lump to the back of his throat. Time, and branches would heal this rip in his heart that had been unexpectedly reopened. For now, he would have to console himself that in other branches, in other times, even if it wasn't in this one, he lived a happy and long life with Louise. He tried to imagine what those would be like. Those branches and times where she still gave him come-to-bed looks, and he could always look forward to another long summer as her lover. She would not be Davey's girl in those branches. Archer supposed he should count himself lucky though. Lucky to be in this branch. After all, if all possible branches existed, then there were some where he had never met her at all.

She would not see all of today, but she wouldn't know why.

It was a sunny spring morning in London. It was early May in 2052, and Louise stepped off the train and made her way towards the teeming Waterloo concourse. She hated this time of the morning, when thousands of fellow passengers navigated their way through to the exits and off to start another day at the office. She herself was heading for a job interview as a researcher at the computer labs at Kings College London. Whether she would get the job, she had no real idea. This was her second interview and she was under no illusion that she could be up against a good many candidates that may be more qualified for the position than she.

She needed a coffee. Perhaps a cappuccino would help her sharpen some blunt edges, make her perform better. She felt into her bag for her purse, pulled it out and looked inside for some change. All that was in there were a few pieces of shrapnel, and no notes. Certainly not enough to buy a coffee in this day and age. She looked around for the nearest cash point machine. She saw one, but the queue was 5 people deep.

Not enough time, she thought. She would have to forgo the coffee and hope that she could dredge some strength and composure from some other unseen well within her.

She headed for the Waterloo Road. Towards an accident. And the people who never lived as a result of her actions, would never have known that she hadn't had the opportunity to save them.

THE DETENTION SPORE

November 2053, and a soft, almost invisible drizzle penetrated the fabric of a morning that was hooded by low, still clouds.

Inside the Axiom Few test-shack, hidden under a motorway over-pass some forty miles outside London, the three members of this small team of freelance techno-graduates stood around the workbench, sipping hot tea, and staring at the metal box that lay upon it.

'It appeared on my kitchen table about two hours ago,' said Davey. 'I think it came through one of your time rips, Geek.'

Geek considered the events of six months before, when an AI from some alternate dimension had utilised his Reflection Goggles to move items through one such rip in order to alter the course of the future. That item had been a simple voucher for free coffee, and its effect had been to save the life of Davey's girlfriend by delaying her from a road accident.

This time the object sent was more substantial. It was a closed metal briefcase with a combination lock on it.

'This was stuck to the lid, but it fell off.' He handed Archer a post-it note. Written on it was a single word.

SHOE

Archer pulled his mobile phone from his pocket and looked at the keypad, where the numbers and digits aligned to enable text messaging. 'So SHOE translates to err... seven, four, six, three.'

Davey smiled. 'Seven, four, six, three, yep. I've already tried that. It didn't work.'

'No, no, you need to look in your shoes,' said Geek. 'Inside your shoes.'

Archer said, 'What for? I think we would have noticed if we had something in our shoes.'

Geek nodded. 'What about on the soles?'

And that was when they found a word and the code. On the sole of one of Archer's Timberlands was the word WATER written in white liquid paper. On the other shoe was a fourdigit code. 'Eight, three, three, one.'

Davey said, 'How did they get there?'

'You know something?' said Archer, 'I have no idea.'

'I don't like this at all.' Davey's hands were shaking as he tapped in the four digits on the combination lock. The final entry brought a tiny pressurised hiss followed by the automated hydraulic opening of the case.

Inside, resting on a moulded foam bedding, were six hypodermic syringes, full of a clear liquid.

Geek leaned closer to inspect the contents of the case. 'Now what do you suppose they are for?'

'And why did someone write WATER on my shoe?' added Archer.

'Somehow I doubt it's water in there.'

'I'm afraid I can't talk about it,' said Archer, placing his glass of wine on the table beside his plate. He looked between the two candles that burned at eye level and caught the cynicism of the look in Gemma's eyes.

'Come on, that's a line,' she said, pausing with a forkful of steak halfway to her mouth. She playfully mocked. 'Your work is top secret. You can tell me but then you'll have to kill me, is that it?'

Archer shook his head, needing to convince her that he wasn't like that, 'It's not like that. Companies force us to sign non-disclosure agreements. Our inventions are pretty fringe. I promise it's not a line.'

Gemma nodded, 'You didn't need a line anyway. I'm already

here. Eating dinner with you.'

Something had caused Geek to sleep late. He rolled over in his bed and looked at the alarm clock. It was nearly eleven AM. He sat up and swung his legs out of bed. God he felt tired. He shuffled into the kitchen and flicked on the kettle. As he rummaged around in the cupboard for a tea bag, his absentminded gaze alighted on the empty glass he had drunk water out of the night before. He picked it up and inspected it more closely. Was that the remnants of a soluble powder scudded up the inside?

The sound of drilling outside the front of the apartment woke Archer up. He had dreamed of a domino game the size of the solar system. Staring up at the ceiling through drowsy eyes, at how the light from between the closed curtains scored a bright sunny line between the window and the door, he realised it must be after eleven AM, as the sun didn't come round the building till then in late Autumn. He pondered for a moment the thrill of the sex he had had with Gemma the night before. Reconnecting with his old girlfriend from school had been quite a rush, despite all the fumbling with that condom.

He had thought he would never see her again after the final day of their exams ten years before. That she had gotten in touch - tracked him down even - was something quite special. Sometimes it really was possible to be lucky in love. He twisted his head to look at her, reaching across in the hope she might be willing to indulge him once more on this fine sunny morning.

But she wasn't there, and before he even bothered to call out, on the off chance she may have gone to make a drink or visit the bathroom, he saw the small pink note that lay on her pillow.

Had to go, sorry. Call me.

He picked up his mobile from the bedside table, swung his legs out of bed and stood up. He pulled up her number and pressed the

Call button.

Voicemail. He left a message. Then he had a shower, dried off, and climbed into jeans and a white t-shirt. But despite half an hour of looking, he couldn't find the Timberland boots he'd worn to the restaurant the night before.

Still rubbing his eyes, Geek wandered through to the hallway to pick up the morning's mail from the doormat. There was only one letter, addressed to him. He paused before opening it and pulled out one single side of typed paper.

Dearest son, I need your help. You have the mind for this sort of thing so I knew I should come to you. To be honest I have no one else to turn to. The question is whether you are prepared to help me. Something strange is happening here...

Geek read the rest of the letter. When he'd finished, he folded it up and placed it back in the envelope, pushing it into the back pocket of his jeans. He was just turning to make his way back to the kitchen when the sound of the loud doorbell shattered the silence, making him nearly jump out of his pale skin. He turned back and opened it. Standing on the doorstep was the postman.

'Forget something did you?' said Geek.

The postman handed him a box, 'Beg your pardon?'

Geek looked at the box. It said "Techipre Components" on the side. It was a delivery of computer parts he'd had on order, 'Thanks very much. Where do I sign?'

'Nowhere,' said the postman as he walked off, shaking his head as though Geek was mad.

Archer's mobile was ringing. He was in the shower, using the meditative power of the fast running water to aid clarity of thought. He was thinking about the strange events of the day before, about the briefcase that had appeared on Davey's kitchen table. But the ringing phone was persistent enough to make him climb out of the shower with shampoo still in his hair, cursing under his breath and hoping it was important. He answered the call, holding the mobile phone away from his wet ear.

'Archer it's me,' said Geek from down the line. 'We need to meet at the test-shack as soon as possible. I know what the syringes are for.'

'That's excellent, what?'

'I'll tell you when we meet. Get Davey. No questions.'

'Give me an hour.'

Geek was holding the letter in one shaking hand. Outside the test shack there was an endless drone of cars on the motorway overhead, and the occasional lorry rumbled past, causing the corrugated iron walls to shake.

'Why should we help him? He's a fraudulent... worm.' he said through clenched teeth as he tossed the letter onto the workbench. 'People like him are the reason why I don't work for corporations. He was a pickpocket with a white collar. He deserved the sentence they gave him, and I hope he never gets out.'

Now Davey spoke, 'Maybe it's not about helping your Dad. For us it's not about saving him. It's about understanding why it's happening in the first place. The virus. The syringes. This stuff is new.'

Archer picked up the folded sheet of paper and started to read again.

Geek turned to Archer, appealing. 'If it was your Dad, Archer. If it was *your* Dad. You wouldn't help him, would you?'

Archer shook his head. 'If it was my Dad. I'd let him rot.'

Geek looked at Davey, happy to have a confirmation of his own sanity from Archer, 'See? Let him rot!'

Archer was scratching his head. 'How does a virus target only criminals anyway? There must be some biological reason.'

Geek had done his research. After he had received the letter he had run some web searches. 'It lends weight to the theory that a chemical imbalance causes people to have criminalist tendencies. Elevated copper and lead in the blood. A zinc deficiency. Hypoglycaemia. Because of intervening social issues - muddying the waters, nature versus nurture etcetera - it's been impossible to tell whether those imbalances actually cause someone to be a criminal. But a virus could be manufactured to target people with those deficiencies.'

'According to your Dad's letter. Nearly all the inmates have the disease, and none of the prison guards.'

'Yeah, and the prison authorities don't seem to give a damn. According to Dad they're happy to let it kill them off. And it's already claimed a handful of lives.'

'It doesn't seem to have gotten out,' added Davey. 'The news of it. Scrub City is obviously keeping tight-lipped on this.'

Archer said, 'I'm not surprised, something like this would cause a media frenzy. So are we agreed that we think there's a Darken Loop involved, except this time we're on the receiving end? Items designed to fix this problem are being sent to us from the future.'

'I think so,' said Davey. 'The syringe briefcase appeared as though it had passed through a rip. One minute my kitchen table was clear, and the next it had a briefcase on it. I didn't see it appear, but nobody had time to sneak in and place it there. It's just like what we did when we sent the coffee voucher.'

'They've got to be the antidote,' said Geek. 'Someone or something is helping us introduce an antidote to the prison, to eradicate the virus. It's like before. We're doing it to save the lives of people who are key to mankind's development in the future. Maybe someone in there...'

'You're talking about prisoners here,' said Davey.

Archer reacted, 'Based on what went before, we knew we were doing overall good. Our actions were endorsed by the Humanity Council and the Space Foundation, we should proceed to do what's required of us.'

'We don't definitely know that what we did was good,' said

Davey, running his hands through his blonde hair.

Archer shook his head, 'But I don't think we should take risks if we're dealing with an artificially intelligent, multidimensional force that is probably many times more resourceful than we are.'

'Resourceful?' Geek laughed nervously. 'If it's so resourceful, why do we keep having to do its bidding?'

That silenced them all. Archer knew perhaps they wouldn't all agree. But that's why they had a leader. 'We should do this,' he said. 'Follow it through. See where we end up, and pull the plug if things start getting out of hand.'

'And has anyone given any thought as to how do we get inside a fortified prison to administer this antidote?' said Geek, his eyes dancing between the two others.

Davey smiled, 'Geek I'm one step ahead of you today. Haven't you worked out what the other word means yet? The other word we found on Archer's shoe?'

Davey arrived back at his apartment a little after four PM. His girlfriend Louise was sitting on the couch watching a crappy daytime soap. She looked up as he walked into the living room. 'You're home early.'

'I was going to say the same thing to you. Everything ok at work?'

'Fine, yes. Everything's fine.' She walked round the sofa, picking up the remote control on the way and turning the volume down. 'In fact, I'm *really* fine.'

She was grinning, and now Davey was nervous. She had a slightly wild look about her.

'I've got something to tell you.' She took another step towards him, a trepidatious one.

'You're pregnant aren't you?'

She threw her hands up, exasperated to have been so transparent. 'How did you guess? I was feeling a little nauseous so I came home and I picked up a testing kit on the way and... How did you guess?'

And Davey let the whole thing run through his head. He intellectualised it. Funny. He had always expected a revelation like that to have more of an impact.

'You don't seem very thrilled,' she said.

And then it started to sink in. A baby. My son, or daughter. Our child. These words. No longer the reserve of other people. He grinned and put his arms around her. 'Are you kidding, it's fantastic! I'm just a little overwhelmed that's all.'

'Me too.'

'Can I see the test?'

She reciprocated in his hug. 'Of course. I'm so glad. This wasn't how I expected it to go though.'

'Expected what?'

'This conversation.'

He hugged her harder. 'Nothing ever does go quite to plan does it?'

She was silent a moment before she said, 'We're going to have a baby.'

He found himself smiling a smile he couldn't stifle. It was the manifestation of his growing excitement. 'I can't stop sm...'

From the bedroom he heard a loud bang, as though someone had kicked a football against the window. They both jumped, and pulled apart from their embrace. 'What the hell was that?'

Davey rushed to the hall and down towards the bedroom, with Louise following close behind. When they arrived they saw a small box, on the floor, leaning against the wardrobe.

'How did that get there?' said Louise, tucking her long brown hair behind her ears, stepping into the room and crouching to get a closer look.

Davey touched her shoulder. 'Don't touch it babe. I know how it got there.'

So Davey had called Archer and Geek back to the test shack. It was past seven o'clock in the evening and the rainy clouds were drain-ing the last light out of a sky that should be brighter.

'Told you I was a resourceful fella,' said Davey, smiling, as he tossed another temporal souvenir onto the workbench.

Geek picked it up. 'Does this mean you'll have to get yourself a job there? To make this work.' He examined it in the light.

Davey nodded, producing a piece of paper from his back pocket. A newspaper article. 'This came with it.'

Geek took the paper and unfolded it. The newspaper cutting was from a classified section, but the cutting did not reveal the date or name of the paper. Ringed in biro, was an advert for a jani-tor's position at the London West Water Treatment Works.

Archer leaned his head in and looked at the picture of Davey, staring out from the laminated badge on the workbench. 'Some-how I don't think it's a fake. And besides, there's the job advert. Davey, I think you need to apply for it.'

'But why should I? We already have the access pass? Why should I apply for the job?'

Geek shook his head, 'I'm not even going down that "causality" road. Let's hope that access badge works in this dimension.'

Davey looked nervous, he knew that it was up to him to use the pass, and do the deed. 'If it was sent to us, then it's bound to work. These things always work, don't they?' Archer didn't reply. Neither did Geek.

'Don't they?' Davey repeated.

Geek rubbed his hands together. 'So now we have all the tools. Kindly sent back to us by well-meaning versions of us and others from future dimensions. We've been given a task. We don't know what it achieves. But we'll do it, because we believe that closing Darken Loops are a good thing, right?'

Archer nodded, perhaps not totally convinced by Geek's pep talk. But that was all Geek seemed to want to say on the matter. Although he needed reassurance, it was ultimately up to Archer.

'Let's do it.'

Davey parked in a deserted lay-by some way down the road from the London West Water Treatment Works; the pumping station that served the prison two kilometres away. He took a deep breath in the silent car before fishing the badge out of his jacket pocket. Looking at it, he contemplated what he knew, and what he didn't know.

Someone had sent him an access pass. It was probably himself, or another version of himself, who had used goggles and rips to get it into his hands. The pass would have come from the future, and probably from a different dimension. But the likelihood was that it would work, as very little was left to chance when it came to closing Darken Loops, or so the Axiom Few believed.

Then there was the job advert, which could only mean that the company hadn't yet taken him on as an employee, because the intention had been for Davey to apply, in order to obtain the pass that would later get sent back in order for him to gain access.

Another loop. Another maddening loop.

He drummed his hands nervously on the steering wheel. The access pass may operate the doors, but if he bumped into someone, a particularly vigilant security guard perhaps, he could be caught, arrested even, and questioned. And even though he had a pass, he still had no right to be there. Cameras were likely to pick him up. The only hope was that his deed will be recognised as a good one when it's understood that he's saving lives.

He looked out at the silent street ahead, waiting for the evening shutdown to kick in, where non-essential streetlights were extinguished to lighten the load on the grid. He was still worried about being spotted. If only Geek could invent a suit that would make him invisible. Some sort of light-distortion jacket. Then he could walk right in there, get the job done, and walk straight out with no fear of being seen. It was a good idea. Perhaps he would suggest it to Geek when he next saw him. That was, if he didn't wind up in the very same prison he was trying to decontaminate.

The streetlights blinked off. Time to go.

He picked up the metal case that lay on the seat beside him, opened the car door, and stepped out into the icy November night.

'Something's puzzling me,' said Geek, drumming his fingers on his kitchen table. He and Archer had been there for over an hour, and Geek's bum was hurting, but he was too nervous to care. On the table sat two empty tea mugs, a take away pizza box with one slice left in it (Archer called this the "polite slice"), and two mobile phones. 'Something not fit?'

Geek nodded slowly, mulling something over in his head. 'Yeah. Something about my Dad's letter. Something about my postman's reaction.'

'Your postman?'

'When he came back to deliver the parcel from Techipre Components.'

'What did he do?'

'Nothing really. He said it didn't require a signature, then went down the steps, but it's just the way he shook his head as he walked away, like he thought I was being an idiot. Why would he think that?'

'You're being paranoid. You're definitely not an idiot. You'd beat him in a pub quiz anytime.'

'Yeah, you're probably right. Like you said, I'm just being paranoid.'

Davey swiped the badge through the security panel. It was a rear entrance so the door only opened to reveal a deserted, dimly lit corridor. Davey entered and looked down at his mobile phone. Geek had uploaded a ZoomSurface schematic of the Water Treatment Works. The dynamic image linked to GPS to provide his position and projected path to the pump room, where he would introduce the contents of the syringes.

Heart racing, ears tuned and listening for footsteps, eyes peeled for cameras, he started to make his way along the corridor.

'What the hell am I doing?' he whispered to himself, 'I must be bloody mad.'

'I hope he's ok,' Archer said in a low, contemplative voice. 'I guess no news is good news right?'

'I doubt it. No news means his phone has been confiscated and he's in a police cell.'

'Thanks for that vote of confidence in the plan.'

'He's risking a lot for us here,' said Geek. 'Risking a lot for the cause of something we know nothing about. Quite bold wouldn't you say?'

Archer was twirling his phone around on the table. 'Yeah, you're right. I'm not sure if I'd have the stones to do what he's doing.'

'Especially as he's going to be a Dad and that.'

Archer's hand slipped and his phone spun off the table, clattering to the floor. 'A Dad?'

Geek smiled thinly, his sideways glance betraying his nervous anticipation of this announcement, 'Yeah, he knew you might not like finding out, what with your history with Louise, so he err... he asked me to tell you.'

Archer sat back, deflated, 'Oh great. Now you're... you don't need to tread on bloody eggsh...'

The mobile phone on the floor started to buzz on the linoleum. Archer sighed and bent to pick it up. He pressed the Speaker button.

'I'm back in the car,' said Davey's voice at the other end.

'I'm coming to you. It's done. Nobody saw me.'

A sharp buzzing noise accompanied the squeal of the metal rollers on the door to Prison Wing 7 at Scrub City. Geek, accompanied by a guard, walked forward into the visitor's area. The guard pointed to a chair and Geek sat and waited for his father.

Archer stretched his legs out on the bed and flicked the remote on the television. An advert for Virgin Galactic trips to the La Luna Space Station was just coming to an end.

Davey arrived home and embraced Louise. He placed his hand on her belly in anticipation of the bump that was to grow there. She smiled at him, and he barely managed to return it. Today, he was plagued by thoughts of Geek's discovery all those months ago. The other members of the Axiom Few knew he had cheated on her. But he also knew the future required that this baby be born. It would grow up to patent a vital piece of AI code.

'I wonder what we'll call him,' he said.

'Or her,' she added, running her hands through his hair.

'Good to see you son.' said Tony from across the cold wooden table.

'I came to tell you that everything will be ok,' said Geek, unable to look directly at his Dad.

Tony laughed quietly, the lines on his face creasing like unironed laundry. 'You took your time to come and say that. I've been here five years.'

Geek smiled nervously and finally met his father's gaze. 'When you wrote the letter...' but he was interrupted by sirens. Building in the distance out of the tiny, wire-mesh covered window near the ceiling of the scummy visitor's room.

'What letter?' said his father, more creases developing on his perplexed face.

'The one asking for our help. You wrote to me.'

Tony laughed. 'I don't think so. You disowned me. You moved to a new apartment.'

What?'

Geek felt a hand on his arm. 'I'm going to have to ask you to end this conversation,' said the guard. 'You need to leave the building immediately.'

'What's going on?'

Tony added, 'You *moved*, son, I don't even know where you live. You never gave me your new address. So I *couldn't* have written to you.'

Geek's mind was racing. Trying to understand. 'What do you mean?'

Then his mobile was ringing in his pocket.

Archer poured some wine from the bottle into the glass. This evening he was drinking a rich red 2039 Chateauneuf du Pape. He rested his head against the headboard as the top headline came on the news.

'Evacuation and quarantine measures put in place at Scrub City. Police and medical experts rush to contain new virus at the prison.'

Archer jolted and spilled his wine over the covers on the bed.

'Shit!'

He reached for his mobile.

'Dammit! Geek. Davey. what have we done?'

Geek was running down the corridor when he finally answered the call. 'Archer, someone's messing with us.'

'I know. I've got Davey on conference. It's on the news. They're locking down Scrub City. Are you out of there yet?'

'I'm getting out as fast as I can. The letter never came from my Dad. Now I understand why the postman was looking funny at me. It was his first visit, not his second.'

He turned a corner and ran down a flight of stairs to the ground floor.

'So the letter was a fake, sent through a rip.'

'Yes, as well as the drug in my glass.'

'What drug?'

Geek had reached the main reception area. A small crowd of people in business attire were being herded out through the main entrance. He followed them into the car park, where a multitude of white vans, ambulances and TV units were parking in jagged formation.

'It was designed to make me sleep late, so I wouldn't suspect any funny business while someone dropped the letter back to my doorstep. Oh boy we really fell for this one guys. How could I have been so stupid?'

'Davey you need to pack your bags and get off-planet,' said Geek as a group of men in biosuits rushed towards him, they were coming from a hastily erected decontamination tent. 'This could swiftly turn into a murder hunt. I have to go.'

Davey was breathless down the line. 'But... Louise. She needs me at the moment. I thought we were saving those people.'

'That baby is the reason all this happened,' said Archer. 'Your baby ultimately causes Brenda to exist and close these loops. You're likely to be in the frame if the authorities ever get round to searching the video footage from the Water Works. And now that you've conceived, now Louise is pregnant, there's no futuristic reason to preserve your relationship with her anymore. We can't guarantee your safety.' 'I'm a murderer,' whispered Davey.

Archer said, 'We need some breathing space. I'm at my computer now. I'm sending you a hyperlink to priority Virgin Galactic flights. Book a ticket, say your goodbyes to Louise and get your arse to Heathrow Base.'

THE VOIDANT LANCE

*First published January 2010,
Jupiter SF Magazine*

Archer was back in the shadow of the Space Foundation Headquarters, wondering what his visit would unearth this time round. It was a bright, clear, crisp winter's day in January of the year 2057. He craned his neck up from where he stood at street level to comprehend the size of the Iceberg Building. The tall glass spire towered above the dynamic London skyline, but he knew that the dark basement levels of the structure ranged into the thousands. Two years ago he'd ventured into those depths, summoned by his father to help with an emergency of apocalyptic proportions. He hoped now that he was here for something less frightening.

With him was Geek, the brains of the Axiom Few; Archer's small band of freelance techno-graduates.

'I know it's hard. Dealing with him,' said Geek.

Archer nodded slowly, composing himself. He often found his work with the Few was at odds with the personal life he struggled to keep at bay. But their business had to come first.

'Let's do it.'

They walked through the automatic doors into the grand reception. Light from an atrium flooded into the space and illuminated a fountain of globes that moved in sync with the planets of the solar system. The only sounds other than rushing water were the echoes of important footfalls that tapped across the expanse of marble floor.

Goddard was waiting for them. Archer's aged father leaned on that same old wooden cane. The result of an injury Archer himself had delivered. Yet again the memory of that fateful night invaded his senses: the night when the two of them had fought each other violently in the confines of a small terraced house in Brighton. That night Archer had, with a bleeding face and racked with despair, leapt into the cold sea, hoping never to be rescued.

Goddard shook Geek's hand but regarded Archer with unhidden hurt when Archer dug his hands into his jeans pockets.

'Very well. Follow me,' said the older man.

They walked towards the lifts and rode up to the twentieth floor in silence, where Goddard's office overlooked the sprawling city that stretched to the hazy West London horizon. As Archer stared out at the shimmering outskirts of the urban-sprawl, he caught sight of a SuperPlane descending towards Heathrow Base, its wings glinting in the unadulterated noon sun.

Goddard motioned for them to sit on one of the sofas in a cosier corner of the office. 'Drink?'

Geek said, 'Thanks I'll have a...'

Archer interrupted, 'He doesn't need a drink. Dad, what's this all about?'

Goddard held his stare for a moment before leaning back against his desk, resting his cane beside him and letting out an audible sigh. 'You are singularly determined to make this difficult aren't you?'

Archer folded his arms and sat back.

'To business, then,' added Goddard. 'Geek, have you been monitoring the Space Foundation web-forums lately?'

Geek shook his head. 'I can't say I have.'

'Well you might do well to. Someone's been posting there for the last seven months under the name Voidant underscore M.'

'Voidant?' Geek sat forward.

Goddard raised an eyebrow. 'Have you heard that word before?'

Archer had heard Geek mention it before. A few years ago while he was sitting in the back of Archer's car, he had been in remote communication with an ultra-intelligent computer called Brenda. In fact, Geek's exact words at the time had been "I've never heard of the Voidant War," in response to something Brenda had said to him. Geek had never disclosed the full content of that conversation. A key part of the Axiom Few's modus operandi was "No questions". Their team worked on a basis of extreme trust.

Archer looked at Geek. Geek held Goddard's inquisitive gaze and said, 'No, I haven't.'

'You're a bad liar, but I will not press you for details. If you want to come forward with them, you will, if you think it necessary. Perhaps I can convince you.' Geek remained expressionless.

Goddard raised his voice, 'Computer?'

'Voice print verified. How can I help you Goddard?' came the smooth female electronic reply, which emanated from speakers around the office.

'Print all threads of the Voidant underscore M forum postings.'

'Printing now.'

Goddard looked at Archer. 'Voidant underscore M refers to himself as the Messenger. His circumstances are contradictory to say the least. He says he is a virtual entity that has existed on earth for seventeen thousand years, waiting for us to develop the technology to enable him to talk to us.

Confusingly, his IP resolution places him off planet, indicating that he has been posting from somewhere on the La Luna orbiting hotel. Virgin Galactic's passenger logs have been scanned but understandably they have no record of anyone using that name to fly to, or from, La Luna. He's a ghost to us.'

Archer shrugged. 'I'm not surprised. So what has this Voidant guy been posting about?'

Goddard retrieved the thin wad of paper from the printer built into his desk and handed them to his son, who proceeded to scan through the forum postings. 'In a nutshell, he's been talking about some sort of object of destruction. He refers to it by a number of names, the "Cleansing Spire", the "Obscurcissez la Tige", or "Darken Rod" in English and the "Torre do Desafio", but mostly he calls it the "Voidant Lance". He says it has different names in different dimensions, if you will.'

'And why haven't you ruled this person out as a crackpot?'

said Geek, though Archer knew full well that Geek was aware of those other dimensions. He had encountered them before. He was clearly trying to deflect any implication that he knew more than he was letting on.

'Because he, or she, makes reference to a number of discoveries that the Space Foundation has not yet made public.'

'What sort of discoveries?'

'Page two, third post down.'

Archer flicked to the second page and read the relevant post.

The Obscurcissez la Tige will impact at the point of the 15th magnetic calibration marker. The position was chosen during the first wave of discussions between the Core Voidant AI Heads and the Fifth Lance Architects. As one of the Lance Architects, I was involved in the design and construction of the markers.

'As you can see, he refers to the Darken Rod in French, and refers to the fifteenth magnetic calibration marker. We searched our database and found an interesting photograph in our Anomalies Archive. Computer, please display Voidant Image Seven.'

'Polarizing windows.' The room darkened.

'Loading image.'

Voidant Image Seven appeared on a screen opposite Goddard's desk. It was a picture taken in bright mottled sunlight of a small stone bridge crossing a dried up brook.

'This is the entrance to L'Ermitage de Collias in the Gard region of Southern France. It's a difficult place to find if you don't know where it is, about three kilometres from the village of Collias, nestled in a forested valley. This is a picture of the roman bridge entering the small remote sanctuary. Computer, zoom in on exhibit four-one-three.'

'Zooming now.'

The image enlarged to show just one single stone embedded in the rock beneath the bridge. Archer could see an engraving on it, though with no real scale to speak of it was difficult to tell its size. Etched into the stone were the words "Voidant MCM-XV".

'Magnetic Calibration Marker Fifteen,' said Archer.

'Notice how the two V-shapes on this engraving are much taller than the rest of the letters,' added Goddard.

'Graffiti,' said Geek.

Goddard uttered a small laugh. 'We've dated this "graffiti" as far back as the eleventh century. Computer, show Voidant Image Twenty Three.'

'Loading image.'

The next image to appear was an infrared picture of a V shaped object on its side. Archer and Geek both twisted their heads to get a clearer idea of what they were looking at.

'This is a near-infrared spectral image of the Voidant Lance. We spotted it yesterday. Just beyond the orbit of Jupiter. It's heading this way from the Upper Scorpius region. Look at Voidant under-score M's final posting this morning. He points out that we should be able to see the Lance by now. We never found out if this person was warning us, or taunting us about our imminent fate. We haven't been able to contact him since.'

Archer was unable to take his eyes off the red glowing image of the triangular shape in the image. 'How big is it?'

'Twenty kilometres from its pointed forward end to its flat rear. It's travelling at thirty-thousand kilometres an hour.'

'So the implication is that the Voidant Lance will impact Southern France?'

'The rotation of the Earth brings the Gard region into position exactly when the Lance strikes, in thirteen days. We've run the mathematics. It's timed to hit the marker dead on. I don't need to tell you what kind of devastation something like that would cause if it hit us. A Krakatoan winter would be a dream scenario under the circumstances. But we would more likely witness tectonic displacement of an immeasurable magnitude. Those who survive the initial shock-wave will have to contend with a compromised food chain, megatsunamis, acid rain, I could go on.'

'How long has it been coming towards us?'

'And why the hell didn't we spot it before?'

'Older images of Upper Scorpius do not show up any anomalies. Our thinking is that it has been cloaked till now.'

'But it must have been launched many many years ago, for the Messenger to have placed an engraved marker in the stone a thousand years ago, and to have claimed to have been hanging around Earth for seventeen thousand years.'

'Questions about Voidant underscore M's intentions, and the form he takes, will have to wait I'm afraid,' said Goddard, taking up his cane and standing before the two seated men. 'What I want to know *now* is whether it's true what they say about your infamous, but elusive, Epoch Bridge.'

Archer drove the car while Geek sat in the passenger seat. They were heading back to the Axiom Few test shack, which was secreted under a motorway overpass some forty kilometres outside London. 'I remember that night Geek.'

'So do I.'

'I never asked you about the Voidant War. But now you need to tell me what's going on.'

'To be honest I don't know. Ever since Brenda, that computer, mentioned the Voidant War I've been searching the web for references to it. I never came across the Space Foundation postings, but I should have known, the Space Foundation lock down their forums to basic keyword searches. It never would have appeared in standard results.'

'Do you think the Epoch Bridge can help us?'

'According to Goddard, the Voidant Messenger referred to the object as the Torre do Desafio. Desafio is Portuguese for Challenge. Challenge Tower. This thing isn't about making us extinct. It's a test, to see if we can survive it. I want to run some more tests on the Epoch Bridge before we make any promises. But if my estimations are correct, and if we can get people into large open areas, stadiums, concert venues, we can vastly increase the amount of people we send over the bridge.'

They arrived at the test shack after the sun had set, as a wintry chill was taking hold of the night and plunging the temperature towards zero. Archer parked the car under the cover of a cluster of trees at the edge of a nearby pine forest. The two of them got out and headed down a grassy bank towards the overpass. The sound of the rush hour cars and trucks grew louder as they approached the test shack, a corrugated metal shed that stood near one of the concrete slopes under the motorway.

'Who's that?' said Geek, pointing ahead.

Archer looked. A small boy was sitting with his back against the shack with his knees pulled up to his chest. He wore a dark coat that was too big for him and as they approached, Archer saw that there was something wrong with the lad. For starters he had no hair, and as he lifted his face to look at Geek and Archer, Archer saw that he had only one eye, the other lid was closed. He also had a harelip and a distorting Habsburg jaw that pushed his chin forward to an abnormal degree.

'What are you doing here mate?' said Archer.

The boy put his hands on the ground beside him and used them at length to stand up. Once erect, although standing in an awkward pose, he brushed the dust off his coat and looked, with his single eye, directly at Geek. When he spoke, his disfigured jaw caused him to slur his words. 'I'm here to stop you from making a big mistake.' 'What mistake?' asked Geek.

'I'm talking about the Voidant Lance. You need to invert your approach. Don't think about saving the people. You have to eliminate the threat. Look. It's cold out here. Can we go inside?'

Inside the test shack, where the Axiom Few tested their inventions to destruction or success, Geek retrieved three cans of BriteStar Fizzy from a small fridge and motioned for the young boy to sit down at the component-strewn workbench.

'Who are you?'

The boy said. 'My name is Lloyd. I'm thirteen. I'm his son.' He was pointing at Archer.

Archer said, 'I don't have a son. I'm not old enough to be your father. Why would you say that?'

Lloyd smiled as best he could given his terrible deformity. 'You told me you'd say that. Look, I don't want to confuse you so let me explain.'

'Please do.'

The boy continued. 'Geek here is planning, right now in his head, to gather large groups of people into stadiums, parks, conference halls, did I leave anything out?' 'Music venues,' added Geek.

'Music venues.' Lloyd rested his hand on a square metallic box that lay on the workbench. The Epoch Bridge he was touching was no larger than a tissue box and had two hand holds on either side.

'Don't touch that,' said Geek.

Lloyd ignored him, 'You've just arrived back from the Space Foundation building in London, haven't you? Geek here knows that if one person holds the two handles on the Epoch Bridge, that person will be sent seventy-eight minutes into the future. You don't know why it's seventy-eight minutes, it just is. What Geek is here to find out this evening, why he's gotten you, Dad, to drive him here, is to find out whether, if *two* people hold hands, and the Epoch Bridge at the same time, they can *both* be sent seventy-eight minutes into the future.'

Archer looked at Geek. Geek nodded slowly. 'He's right. That was going to be my suggestion. I want to know if it works for more than one person. Lloyd, how do you know all this?'

'Let me save you all the trouble. The experiment works. You will tell the Space Foundation later tonight and they will start mass-producing these things. They'll turn over every factory they control to the construction of Epoch Bridge units. In thirteen days when the Voidant Lance crashes through the Earth's atmosphere you will have executed a plan to gather as many people as you can into large spaces, holding hands, a human chain looping back to an Epoch Bridge in each location. Twenty million units will be made. This... oh so wonderful device...will bounce three and a half billion people seventy-eight minutes into the future at the exact moment the Voidant Lance strikes L'Ermitage de Collias. We will be saved from the initial blast, a shockwave that would devastate buildings and people, displace continents and oceans. You couldn't save us from the century-long winter that would follow, but avoiding the blast is a good start.' Lloyd raised his arms and yelled sarcastically, 'Praise the Lord! You are the saviour.'

Archer spoke, 'Somehow you don't seem convinced, Lloyd.'

Lloyd's eye was dark. He folded his arms and spoke sternly and with spite. 'You thought you were saving the human race. You were killing us! We became... we will become... genetically scarred, as well as having to face a four-degree drop in temperature that's set to plunge us into another ice-age living under sulphur-dioxide clouds. Perhaps it would be better to let us all die in the impact after all.'

'We haven't got the time to test it,' said Geek. 'The only reason the Space Foundation came to us is because they have no other options on the table. That's why they *always* come to us.'

'You didn't *test* the Epoch Bridge enough. This unit you designed to save us all, introduces mutations, anomalies into our genetic structure. You mess up your DNA. You introduce cancers and create aberrations. Eventually, some twenty years from now, after it's all too late, Geek here will perfect a module for the Epoch Bridge to enable *backwards* travelling. It took twenty years to nail the code, and I was the one who volunteered to come back to tell you that you picked the *wrong solution* this time. You sent yourselves this message from the future. I'm the one delivering it to you. Sorry it didn't work out.'

'What other solution is there? What else can we do?'

'Don't you get it? You still use the Epoch Bridge. But you don't use it on the people. You use it on the Lance.'

Archer was silent.

'Dad. Your own Dad messed you up. You hate him for what he did to you all those years ago. I don't... Look Dad, don't make it a running joke.'

Geek was waving his hands around like an animated scientist who was explaining the success of his latest experiment. Archer smiled at the analogy, because it wasn't actually an analogy at all. 'The leading point of the Voidant Lance tapers to the width of a pinhead,' said his Axiom Few partner from the podium. 'We've all seen it in the pictures. My original Epoch Bridge prototype would only bounce organic matter into the future. I have spent the last three days devising an updated version of the unit that can now bounce inanimate matter forward instead.'

Archer looked around Conference Room Four on the sixth floor of the Space Foundation HQ. The room was currently host to two hundred and fifty assembled scientists. Many of them were respected in their fields, but all of them had their hands tied by corporate budgets and dogged approval processes that they would never be able to develop something as mind-blowing as the Epoch Bridge. This was the Axiom Few's leading edge.

'Now that we can do this, I propose not to bounce the people forward, but to send the Lance itself seventy-eight minutes into the future, so that it misses the Earth entirely. And here's how.'

Geek clicked a button on his presentation controller, and an object shaped like a complex funnel appeared on the screen.

'What's the world like, post impact?'

Archer and Lloyd sat on plastic school chairs retrieved from the inside of the test shack. They were cooking sausages on barbeque forks over a small fire. Archer hadn't yet decided if he would take Lloyd back to his apartment. He lived alone, but what were the risks of other people seeing the boy and asking questions? He would make that decision with Geek when he returned from the Iceberg Building, where he was developing the object he called the Attachment.

Looking at his son, trying to come to grips with the fact that this boy was even sitting here, Archer hoped against hope that Geek's Attachment worked.

Lloyd's face was distorted further by the shadows caused by the licking flames, but it reverted his countenance to a primal beauty that Archer found disquieting. The boy's mutated features drove home the sincerity of his plight. Above them a swirling vista of stars in the sky was made visible by the evening shutdown, where streetlights were extinguished to conserve the power grids. Only a handful of people knew that the beautiful space above them concealed an alien menace that the Axiom Few and the Space Foundation were struggling to understand.

'I can't speak for those who survived the first few years,' said Lloyd, 'but the sunsets of my early childhood were stunning. Reddy orange dust scoring across darkened skies, interspersed with vertical uplifts, where huge fans were built at great expense to push the accumulated dust out into space. Mutations were prevalent in the newborns. Geek would have found that the monkeys he bounced through the Epoch Bridge would give birth to abnormal offspring, if they'd had the chance.'

Archer shook his head, trying to see the image of this dark future world they were on the cusp of creating.

'Vast underground cities were built. Society was on the rebuild but only after devastating collapse. Anarchy and crime prevailed. We were back in the Stone Age, let alone the Ice Age. If only we'd had more time.'

'Couldn't we send you back further, to give us a longer warning?'

Lloyd shook his head. 'Geek never got the chance to augment the backward bridge technology. He died soon after perfecting the module I used. Twenty year Epochs were all we could manage.'

'God. I never would have thought we'd be responsible for so many deaths.'

'Blame the Voidants. Rumours began to surface that now they'd laid waste to the place, they were in a position to take over. I can't think why they'd be interested in a dust ball like Earth. The rumours were that a war was on the horizon. I don't know if I believe all that. People were apt to jump to conclusions and make up stories.'

'The Voidant War is real.'

Lloyd stared at him. 'How do you know?'

Archer shook his head, 'I just do.'

The driver of the Space Foundation SUV honked the horn as they crawled through the masses of people assembled on the road that led up to the summit of Mont Ventoux. Riding in the back of the vehicle were Archer and Lloyd. The police escort that cut them a path up ahead did nothing to stop the throngs from returning to the road and banging on whatever part of the vehicle their fists could access, and Archer found it unnerving.

Geek had deployed himself to the city of Nimes to oversee the mounting of the Attachment to the old Hind Mi-24 Helicopter Gunship that was going to intercept the Lance above L'Ermitage. The only other member of the Axiom Few, Davey, was stationed on La Luna, to get the best view there was of the approaching destroyer of worlds.

The Giant of Provence stood at an altitude of almost twothousand metres and on this beautifully clear day, news of the destruction of mankind had brought millions to the mountain to get the best view of the end of the world. It would undoubtedly be spectacular.

Archer wore one of Geek's ComArcs, a low latency headset that provided beautiful voice clarity within an encrypted subnet. Davey paged him from his own ComArc on La Luna.

'Archer this thing is beautiful. We're tracking it through telescopes and it's coming for us at one hell of a lick.'

He thought of the images and videos he had seen of the Lance. A dark, almost organic looking V-shaped structure with immense shifting panels on all four sides of its elongated pyramid shape: menacing in its relentless journey towards Earth's delicate surface.

'I hope Geek and his Space Foundation buddies have got all their calculations right,' he said, unable to keep a quiver from his voice.

Geek interjected. 'We've run the calcs a million times. I have faith in the mathematics and the best minds on the planet have verified the sums. This is *going* to work. But I have work to do so if you guys will stop talking and let me concentrate,' he chuckled at his own irony, 'I might be able to save a few lives today.'

One hour later Archer and Lloyd were at the summit of Mont Ventoux, surrounded by huge crowds, but held within a fenced compound set up by the Foundation and protected by guards to keep some of the rowdier people at bay. A row of telescopes had been set up to enable them to see all the way across Provence, beyond Avignon, and some eighty kilometres to where Geek's plan would play out. All they could do now was watch with the world as a thousand cameras pointed at the area of blue sky above L'Ermitage de Collias.

'Trois minutes!' boomed a voice over a PA system that had been installed for the occasion. Archer's heart pumped thickly in his chest and he looked down to see Lloyd was gripping his hand. He hadn't even noticed the boy take it. Everyone else was looking at the sky but there was no sign of the Lance yet. Archer knew that the giant object would not be visible until the last few seconds, and then it would all be over in an instant, one way or the other.

He started to feel sick. 'Geek, talk to me.'

Geek responded instantly, his breathing was laboured, 'The Gunship is in place above the marker stone. You should be able to see it.'

Archer looked through the telescope, which had been previously trained to the precise location the remote-controlled Gunship would hover. A little tweaking of the focus brought the bulky helicopter into view. On top of the Gunship was Geek's Attachment, the wide funnel that protruded from the top of its forward rotor. It made the helicopter look top-heavy.

'Deux minutes!'

'Where are you now?'

Geek was out of breath. 'I'm on the Tour Magne. It's a Roman hill-top tower in Nimes. We've just climbed about three hundred steps to get a better view.'

The familiar sound of a cane clicking behind Archer was soon followed by the appearance of Goddard. Lloyd looked up at him and said, 'I want you both to know that if this all goes wrong, I won't hold it against you.'

Goddard smiled and put his hand on the boy's shoulder, looking at Archer he said, 'Nice to see that the dry wit runs in the family. What I want to know is, do *you* still hate me Archer? We could be two minutes away from extinction, so I thought now would be a good time to make peace.'

Archer regarded him for a handful of seconds before shaking his head, cursing himself for even considering extending an olive branch to the man, 'Geek's plan will work Dad, and then I would regret it. It's *you* that needs to make peace.'

'One minute!' and then all eyes found their way to telescopes and binoculars. Archer, Lloyd and Goddard looked to the skies. There was a rise in the commotion of the crowd and some people started to yell and scream and even cheer and sing as their hysteria escalated.

Archer heard Geek say, 'Gunship position holding. Davey, what do you see?'

'I'm glad I'm not down there with you. This thing is massive. I don't know what else to say. It's beautiful, but it's coming straight for you. And I can see France and Spain and the Med and it looks like the flight plan the Messenger told us about tallies and... this is... the biggest damned thing that ever went past me. Whoa! Hang on. Did you see that?'

'See what?' said Archer and Geek at the same time, but Davey was already speaking over them.

'There are creatures on this thing; living creatures. A seething bloody mass of things. Crawling across. They're disgusting. We can see them. I thought you said this thing was inanimate.'

Archer yelled into the ComArc. 'The shifting panels weren't mechanical. Geek you said you recalibrated for inorg...' Archer couldn't get the words out. Terror swept over him as he realised the implications of having altered the Epoch Bridge to bounce only inanimate matter into the future. It was beginning to look like Geek's Attachment would be completely useless. He yelled Geek's name into the ComArc and he yelled it again but Geek didn't respond. His colleague was too busy shouting at someone next to him. 'Establish the connection. Get the old code ready. Dammit! Hurry, we've run out of time...'

Archer looked down at Lloyd. Lloyd said, 'Are you okay Dad?'

'Thirty seconds,' came the voice over the loudspeakers.

Archer stumbled over his words. 'Lloyd, Dad, I'm so sorry. I think we've made a terrible mistake.'

Geek was shouting in his ear. 'Connect, for the love of... Please connect.'

'Twenty seconds,' shouted that persistent voice, calling away the seconds to their inevitable death. Archer's hands rose to his damp sweaty face and he barely heard himself whispering. 'How could we have got it so *wrong*?'

Then Davey said, 'I'm sorry too,' and Archer realised that at least one member of the Axiom Few would survive this day of doom. But for what?

'Ten seconds.'

Geek was shouting 'Yes! Yes! Now upload it. Now!'

And those remaining seconds slowed down to nothing. Archer stared into the distance through the hazy sun and wondered if the replacement code would get to the device in time. The taste of impending death rose like sick bile in his throat. His heart ceased to beat, and his eyes focused to the tightest tunnel. A dark tunnel of shame and defeat.

Then a flare of fire burst into the sky above the Gard and it all happened in moments. The Lance dipped out of the blue on its relentless downward plunge. The screams grew to hysterical levels as the object crashed through the stratosphere, awash with flame. The dark spike glowed red as it fell to the Earth, ripping the day apart with a brutal, earsplitting rumble.

The ComArc channel had been silent. Archer knew there was no point in even speaking to Geek or Davey during this final fraction of time. Either the Attachment would work or it wouldn't and there was nothing he could do about it now. He barely heard Geek whispering through tight teeth, his voice riddled with quivering fear, 'Now *execute!* Good God Almighty.'

Archer leaned into the telescope eye-piece just in time to see the fine tip of the Torre do Desafio connecting with the Gunship's Attachment. For a split second Archer visualised it crashing right through, disintegrating the Gunship and impacting with the delicate green planet, but then he saw the reality. The Voidant Lance winked out of existence.

The air that rushed in to take the place the huge threat had just vacated buffeted across the vineyards of Provence in a chorus of mini tornados. Apparently it spoiled the grapes and eliminated that year's wine harvest.

After all the planning, the mistakes and the terror, the spectacle was over in the shortest moment, and Archer began to breathe. Seventy-eight minutes later, the Voidant Lance and an unmanned helicopter Gunship reappeared out in space and continued on a journey to nowhere.

Planet Earth was untouched by the Voidant attack this time. But Archer wondered if there were more threats on their way. He already knew that there were intelligences out there with harmful intentions. And he supposed that provided humanity had sufficient warning, they might just be able to do enough to stop it wiping life off the face of the Earth.

Standing on a pier in the seaside town of Brighton in the lonely dawn hours, Lloyd said, 'Thanks Dad. Thanks for giving me a better chance. Now I can remove myself.' He cocked a thumb towards the wintry English Channel. 'I can jump off like you once did.'

They were both silent. Archer wanted to say so many things to the boy, but nothing came out.

Lloyd continued, 'It's not fair that your Dad blamed you for your Mum's death. She died giving birth to you, but it wasn't fair for him to hold that against you. I can understand why you fell out. I understand why you fought. But can't you ever forgive him?'

'I'll try to do it, for you. I'm beginning to see the importance of family.'

Lloyd smiled.

'You don't have to go,' said Archer. 'I don't want you to leave.'

'You have to let me do this. You will fall in love in a few years time and you will marry her and have me again. But I can't be here twice. I'm not needed anymore.'

Archer nodded. 'What's her name?'

'Come on Dad,' Lloyd was grinning mischievously. 'You know I can't tell you that.'

And with that, Archer's son turned and leapt into the unforgiving sea.

Before the boy had even hit the folding turbulent water, Archer's mobile phone started to ring. He let it be for a few moments but it was persistent. He eventually raised it to his ear.

'It's me...' said Goddard at the other end.

'Look Dad, I...'

'Listen to me. Listen to me carefully. We've tracked another two-hundred and seven Lances, all inbound.'

'My God.'

'Is Geek with you?'

'No, he's...'

'Then *get him*. We have no time to spare.'

THE TECHIPRE FILAMENT

London 2058, and the sun beat down on the tinted windows of the Space Foundation Lounge in Terminal 8 of Heathrow Base. Outside, across the endless tarmac, superplanes glinted as they lined up for runway 27, and VTOL's taxied serenely out to the Column. Archer was lost in the silent manoeuvres going on beyond the windows when the sliding doors opened behind him. He snapped his head round to see who had entered the space, doubling its occupancy.

It was Geek, the brains of their team of freelance technograduates. The younger man was wearing his stock white Axiom Few t-shirt, a low slung pair of jeans and scratty black converse trainers with flapping, untied laces. A sizeable rucksack was slung over one shoulder, causing his thin body to tilt to compensate. He hurried to the chair opposite Archer and slumped into it, out of breath. 'Does anyone know why we're here?'

'Dad and I had to cut short our golfing trip,' said Archer. 'He's over in one of the Space Foundation offices sorting out some paperwork. He didn't say much on the flight down from St Andrews. Only that he wanted to talk to us all together.' 'Did your Mum fly down with you?'

Archer shook his head. 'She's still up there at the health spa, with a couple of her friends.'

The lounge doors slid open again and Archer's father strode quickly into the room, brandishing four boarding passes. 'Sorry about the wait.' He shook Geek's hand, 'Thanks for coming at such short notice. The Space Foundation are always grateful for your...'

'It's ok Goddard,' said Geek. 'I wasn't up to much today anyhow. Where are we going?'

Goddard looked to Archer. 'Any sign of Davey yet?'

'He called a few minutes ago to say he was just entering the Base. He had to drop Gemma home. They were spending the weekend in the Isle of Wight. It's their wedding anniversary.'

Goddard's eyes drifted momentarily to the floor, 'I'll have to make it up to them. And what about you son? Is there any sign you and Louise might tie the knot. She's good for you.'

Geek nodded in agreement. 'It's probably about time mate. She might not wait forever.'

Archer stared once more out of the window, as the spinning radar beyond the terminals plotted the positions of local air traffic, manoeuvring things into position. Although he felt slightly embarrassed by their interest in his love life, he tried not to let it show. 'I've been thinking about it. Maybe after this trip. Maybe I'll...'

He was rescued from saying any more by the buzzing of his mobile phone. It was a text message from Davey, saying that he'd parked up and was on his way. Archer showed the phone screen to his father.

'We'll meet him on the way out,' said Goddard. 'Get your things. Our VTOL is waiting.'

The VTOL accelerated heavily during its climb to a cruising altitude of fifty kilometres, crossing the threshold of land and sea somewhere over the southern coast of Cornwall. Archer stared out at the expanse of the sinking world as the four passengers of this luxury Space Foundation VTOL toured through brilliant white and striking blue, as vertical structures of cumulonimbus clouds loomed around them during their ascent. The clouds dropped well below them as they ate a light lunch over the Bay of Biscay, and soon after, over coffee and orange juice, the darkness of space at the edge of the Earth's atmosphere crowned the world as their conversation turned to the matter at hand.

'We're going to Ascension,' said Goddard. 'It's a small island just south of the equator in the middle of the Atlantic Ocean between

Africa and South America. It's home to the Wideawake Air Force base and, frankly, little else. The island is a British territory but the base is owned by the US, and used extensively by the British. It's a volcanic island, and it's under threat.'

'We're not geologists,' said Geek.

'Volcanologists,' corrected Davey.

Goddard raised his hand pleading silence. 'Six months ago, the Techipre Electronics Company was contracted by the US and UK governments to build a solar power plant on Ascension, to provide electricity to the base. They started a month ago and while they were digging the foundations for their cell farms, they came across an anomaly. An object buried a kilometre below ground.'

'What sort of object?'

Goddard took a sip of his coffee, 'A perfect sphere. Computer, please display Ascension Live Sat Image.'

'Voice print verified,' came the electronic reply, over speakers buried in the plane seats. 'Polarizing windows.'

Outside, the remaining light from the sky diminished to blackness and a screen rolled down at the front of the cabin.

Onto the screen came a satellite image of Ascension Island, an orange and green, almost triangular shaped blob, in the centre of a rich blue sea, with white surf cutting around the edges of the jagged land.

'Ascension Island. Size approximately ninety-one square kilometres. Used by the Space Foundation as a range telemetry station for equatorial space launches from the US and Africa. Ascension is important to us. It enables British planes to refuel on the way to the Falklands, which keeps our presence on those islands assured. As you know there have been two wars with Argentina over the Falklands over the last century. The Falklands are our foothold in the Antarctic, so Ascension is critical for that to happen. The US use Ascension when they engage in European and African theatres of war, so the island has collaborative Allied strategic importance. Computer zoom to base.'

The sensation of descending to the island was nauseous but fleeting as the image zoomed to show a portion on the western side.

'We'll be staying at the Wideawake barracks here. The sphere itself is two kilometres northeast, at this dig site.' 'All I can see is rough ground,' said Davey.

'We're masking the dig in real-time. We don't want the actual image getting out to the web. I'm just showing you the location for now because, as you can see from where I'm pointing, it's nested between two ridges in the nearby valley. There's been some geological compression along this faultline here over the centuries. And more recently, some minor tremors over the last few....'

'Like I already said,' Geek persisted. 'We're not geo...'

Goddard raised a hand. 'All you need to know is that it's unstable, and that marks the end of your geology lesson for the day. Right now I suggest you get some sleep. We arrive in two hours, and then we'll be going straight to the Techipre site to meet with the team who found the sphere. It's going to be a long day.'

'Can you say what has this got to do with us, Dad?'

Goddard shook his head. 'I'm afraid I don't know. All I do know is that I've had orders from the Prime Minister that you three are to be brought to Ascension as soon as possible, and that the Space Foundation is to spare no expense in getting you there. Believe me, I want to know what this is about just as much as you do.'

The shadows were long in the reddening evening sky as the VTOL descended through layers of cirrus clouds to the Column at the Wideawake Base. Archer stared out at the view as the red volcanic ground reared up to meet them, to swallow their craft into its undulating folds. Gleaming white satellite dishes pointed vertically skyward, underlining their equatorial location by communicating with geosynchronous satellites hanging in space directly above their heads. The new moon rising in the east revealed its crescent at a new angle, a sad mouth that perhaps, on some celestial level, knew the amount of heartache that would later happen here.

Such symbolism was lost on an unwitting Archer as the four men deplaned and rode a van to a holding pen. They watched and waited while their passports were verified and papers were signed. The VTOL, despite its cost and requirement for constant use, was towed to a hangar to wait for the Axiom Few to return to the base for their homeward trip. And all the time Archer wondered why they had been summoned to this remote location at such an inevitably high price-tag.

The opportunity to shower and change clothes at the barracks was swift, and as the rich red sky darkened to night Archer, his father, Davey and Geek boarded an army minibus which drove them out to the site of the sphere. The road was winding and crested over soft, dark hills. They rode in tired silence. Twenty minutes later they descended into a manmade crater no more than a kilometre across, where hastily constructed scaffolding and portacabins encircled the huge smooth metallic sphere, half buried in the red earth. As the men exited the minibus, each of them uttered the superlatives that sprung to their minds but all were inadequate for describing the immensity and scope of the striking dome that they were looking at.

Striding over to them at a brisk pace was a thin man dressed in dockers, a blue shirt and Timberland boots caked with Ascension dust. The equatorial night was warm and so everyone seemed to want to roll up the sleeves on their arms. Goddard shook the man's hand, grabbing his forearm with the other hand in a way that told Archer these men had good history together. Goddard gestured to The Axiom Few, 'This is my son Archer, his colleagues Davey and Geek. Guys, this is Miles. He's heading up the Techipre solar project here on Ascension, and he's the man who alerted the Space Foundation to the existence of the sphere.'

'Pleased to meet you all after all this waiting. I've heard a lot about you guys. I must admit, I'm jealous of where you are. Operating on the edge, still able to invent without the corporations breathing down your neck. To still be able to do that, and call your own shots... Well you must be good. Would you like a drink?'

'We've come a long way Miles,' said Archer. 'We've put our lives on hold for this, and we still don't know why. Perhaps we can just get straight down to business.'

'Then allow me to explain, over a drink,' Miles persisted. 'Bring these travellers a beer.'

'As Goddard has already told you, we found this object while we were digging the foundations for our solar cells. Geologists tell me that it's been buried here in undisturbed strata for twenty to thirty thousand years. The sphere itself is solid but for two discrepancies, at least, two that we've found so far.'

'What sort of discrepancies?'

Miles pointed towards the dome. 'Over there is a man-sized door. Can you see it? The line around it is just visible.'

In the fading light Archer could just make out the rectangular edge Miles was referring to. Next to it stood two armed officers.

'Has it been opened?'

'We can't open it from this side.' Miles shook his head. 'It hasn't opened. We've had cameras trained on that door since we unearthed it, and guards beside it all the time.'

'And what's the other thing you mentioned? The other discrepancy?'

'A small light. A small flashing light, a little way further round the dome, just out of our line of sight from here. Now the light we've been able to make more of.' Geek spoke. 'Flashing you say. Binary?'

Miles nodded. 'A binary light. Pulsing out messages in a basic numeric to alpha cryptogram. A equals one, B equals two, and so on. It's been looping a set of words and phrases constantly for the last 3 days, since we started to understand what we were dealing with.'

'And what has this got to do with us?'

Miles uttered a small laugh. 'Haven't you figured it out yet? You're the Axiom Few, and the sphere has been asking for you.'

'We're calling it the streamcode,' said Miles as he passed a printout to Geek, who read it and passed it to Archer, who took it and read the words himself.

*BiologicalRetroEnabledNthDimensionalArray
StructureCeresKhartoumIcebergPrecipiceVoidant
VoucherVoidantAxiomFewAxiomFew
InmateAutumnVirusCriminalGeneticGenetic
AxiomFewBringAxiomFewAscension
7'56S14'22W7'56S14'22W7'56S14'22W*

Miles continued, 'This streamcode has been looping for three weeks, like I said. The numbers at the end are the coordinates of Ascension but, does any of the rest of it make any sense?'

Archer handed the paper to Davey and shook his head. 'I've no idea what any of this means. What about you guys?' The two of them stared blankly back at him.

'Funny thing is,' said Miles, his gaze seeming to diffuse absently into the distance, as though he was trying to understand the implications of what he was saying. 'As soon as your VTOL entered Ascension airspace, the sphere stopped speaking to us.'

Goddard spoke up, 'So we can only hope that now the Few are here, it'll move into the next phase of its communication.' Miles was still looking absently over Archer's shoulder, but then Archer realised he was actually focussed on the sphere behind him. 'Erm, I think it's already started.'

They all looked in the direction of Miles's gaze, at the black rectangular hole which now existed where the door once was. The entrance had appeared so silently that the armed guards who stood sentry in front of it hadn't even noticed.

Geek was peering into the gaping black entrance, but he quickly turned to the others and said, 'Who's volunteering?'

Davey laughed nervously, 'Not you then I guess.'

Archer stepped forward and looked inside. 'Get me a torch.'

Miles put a hand on Archer's arm. 'Do want a soldier to go with you? One with a big gun?'

Archer considered the possibility of a gung-ho approach for a moment, 'Whatever this thing is, I don't think we want to antagonise it, do you? If it's been asking for us, then I hardly think it's going to wipe me out at its first opportunity.'

Miles nodded. 'Fair point.'

The bottom of the entrance was at knee height so it only required a high step for Archer to climb into it. He took the torch that was held out to him by the soldier with the gun, and turned towards the hole beyond. 'Don't wait up.'

And with that he swung the beam of light to illuminate the way ahead.

Which was actually not all that far. The smooth featureless metallic walls continued a mere ten metres along a corridor before terminating. The way forward was blocked by another wall. Archer's thoughts were now enveloped in the concept of whether the sphere was a spacecraft, spherical and perfectly aerodynamic in any direction, or some other unknown contraption.

He stepped forward. Set into the wall at the end of the corridor was a small dark rectangle at head height that could have been a viewing port. Archer made his way towards it and put his eyes to the rectangle. He switched off the torch at his waist to remove any glare.

At first he saw nothing but black through the small window. But as his eyes adjusted to the purity of the darkness he began to realise that he was looking into the entirety of the hollow sphere. There was nothing specifically tangible about that feeling, as he had no sensory information to back it up. But instinct created and reinforced the sensation of an expanse nonetheless.

Then he saw something, seemingly floating in the centre of the artificial cavern. He stared at it for a few moments before understanding what it was. Two small clamps holding between them what looked like a thick piece of wire; a filament. It was difficult to assess the size of the objects given his lack of a frame of reference, but he would have guessed that the whole unit was no more than a couple of metres across, and about half a kilometre away in the centre of the room.

The unit flashed, as though it was now aware that it had a spectator. The filament seemed to ignite to momentarily light up the large room which curved downwards and upwards in equal measures. With this change in state came images, painted on the wide concave inner walls of the sphere. Somehow Archer saw them all, as though those same images had also been engraved onto a part of his brain, scoring images into his mind like hieroglyphics in stone. And with each piece of the carving he began to understand. Invaded with information before the darkness returned, his brain seemed to burn with heat and he stumbled back. Backwards along the rumbling, trembling corridor, towards the entrance of the sphere. Backward into the arms of his father and Davey, who caught him as he stumbled over the lip of the doorway. The last thing he heard before passing out was the armed guard yelling "AVALANCHE!"

Daylight streamed in through the mosquito blinds on the windows when Archer opened his eyes. It took him a few moments to realise he was not in London. No. He was on Ascension; on a bottom bunk bed in a sparsely furnished room in the army barracks. His father was sitting in the chair opposite the bed. The older man was holding a mobile phone. When he saw Archer looking at him he started to send a text.

'I'm telling them you're awake.'

'I saw something,' said Archer.

'What did you see?'

'Something terrible. Another life. Other lives. On the walls. I saw other versions of me.'

Goddard nodded, 'Geek's been looking at the sphere. He saw a device in the centre. No doubt you saw it too. He's been working with the Techipre scientists to try and figure out what it is.'

'I saw things that never happened.'

'Right after your adventure last night that binary light started up again.'

Archer sat up. 'The sphere is communicating again? The same streamcode?'

Goddard stood and walked over to the bed. 'Not the same streamcode. No. A new one.'

Archer rubbed his eyes. 'One of the things I saw was us alone.'

'Alone?'

'Dad we were alone, standing at Mum's grave. Mum was dead. She'd died in childbirth. She lost too much blood. It devastated you.'

Goddard smiled thinly, apologetically. 'I can assure you she's absolutely fine.'

'And I hated you. I felt the hate. Why would I hate you?'

Goddard rested a soft hand on Archer's shoulder. 'You're the best son a man could ever ask for. I could never imagine a world where you hated me. I think it would destroy me if we weren't the greatest of friends.'

Archer nodded, acknowledging the sincerity in his father's eyes. 'I saw other things too. Versions of my life where Louise wasn't with me. It made no sense. It would kill me if I lost her.'

'Then when we return to London, you must *secure* that. You must make sure you ask her.'

Archer felt a flutter in his chest. Was it the sickness and excitement of love and lust germinating there? Had those emotions been magnified by his experience in the sphere? 'I wish she was here.'

'Do you want me to call ahead to Tiffany's Jewellers? Book an appointment?'

Archer nodded. 'I feel that loss so palpably. The loss of Louise in those images, even though it didn't happen. It's like a strong dream. You know how they can really... really affect you?'

'Especially if you're close to waking.'

'Why would that thing out there show me those images?'

'I don't know.'

'When I was at school, back in Brighton, there was this girl I had a crush on, and so did quite a few other boys in my class. She was beautiful, but out of my league. One night I dreamed that I kissed her. I kissed her through a gap in a chain link fence. And there was something about the memory of that kiss, superimposed onto her from the reality of some other kiss I'd had, that hollowed me out. For the whole of the following day I felt this profound sense of loss. I had experienced something so vividly in my head. Knowing the dream would just have to do, because I would never get to experience kissing her in real life. Funny thing is, that dream was probably more vivid than any reality that might have moved in to replace it.'

'Don't dwell on things that haven't happened, Archer. Perhaps you're learning the consequences of not seizing the moment. Come on, let's get back to the site.'

Archer and Goddard returned to the sphere. In the bright morning sunshine the dome looked like some sort of highconcept museum exterior. The smooth wide curve of the metallic roof shone brilliantly against the dull red rock of Ascension. Last night, Archer had not been able to see how high the two ridges from the satellite picture really were. To the north and south the promontories soared some fivehundred feet above them, framing the valley in which the sphere sat buried. The two ridges almost seemed to Archer like a gateway, or great protectors of some profound technical truth.

Miles was carrying a document wallet at his waist when he came to meet Archer and Goddard near the entrance to the sphere. He shook their hands and wasted no time on giving an update.

'After you passed out, there was an avalanche. Part of the ridge to the north collapsed into the valley below.'

'Was anyone hurt?'

'Thankfully no, it was nowhere near any habitation or anything. But the source of the displacement was the sphere itself. That thing caused it. We've seen previous avalanches in the area. Something about that sphere has created a sizeable geological instability. We'd only suspected it till now.'

Archer said, 'Dad mentioned the binary light has started up again. What's it saying now?'

Miles gave a wry smile and pulled a printout from his document wallet. 'You might not want to read this.' Archer took it and read the single repeated line.

ArcherOnlyArcherOnlyArcherOnly
ArcherOnlyArcherOnlyArcherOnly
ArcherOnlyArcherOnlyArcherOnly
ArcherOnlyArcherOnlyArcherOnly

Geek snatched the sheet of paper and scrunched it into a ball, 'This is crap. We should go. You don't owe this lot anything.'

Archer smiled. 'It's ok. Aren't you intrigued about all this? Don't you want to know what this device is?

Geek stared across again at the hulking dome, glinting in the bright day. 'Yeah, of course I'm interested. But I don't like all this printout stuff. Asking for us. Asking for you. It's not going to lead to anything good. We all know that. Don't you feel like a lamb being brought to the slaughter? At the whim of the Prime Minister of all people. You've never been one to follow the fucking establishment.'

'My curiosity is what's driving me here. Not some government agenda. Can someone tell me what we're dealing with here?'

Miles spoke, 'We've trained our instruments on this thing and we've detected some interesting stuff. Gravitational fluctuations.'

'We've spotted bosonic forces and fermions in there,' added Geek.

'Which means it's a closed, stable, supersymmetrical system. What exists inside that sphere is beyond the range of our scientific capabilities.'

Geek dug his hands into his pockets, 'In other words, noone on this earth would be able to make one of these things.

Scientists have been trying to create what's going on inside there for about fifty years and we still haven't cracked it.'

'That object in the middle,' Miles added. 'That wire, is under excitation. Like a guitar string under tension.'

'It's vibrating, in an eleventh dimensional, M Theory sort of way,' added Geek.

Archer struggled to keep the awe from his voice, 'So it's a pretty intense piece of kit.'

Miles shook his head quickly. 'You're not wrong. The energy source from the vibrations isn't from here.'

Archer cast his eyes to Geek for more reassurance, and found it written in his colleague's eyes. 'Isn't from here?

Geek nodded. 'I don't know where the casing came from, Archer, but the bit in the middle isn't from this dimension. It can't be.'

Miles continued, 'Something from another dimension is using this device to communicate with you. I don't know, perhaps the string membranes, the dimensions, are touching, allowing that wire to transmit data between.'

Archer raised his hands. 'I'm tired of the speculation guys.' That silenced them. He said no more. This time he was going to get to the bottom of it all. No more passing out. He turned and hoisted himself up into the man-sized entrance to the dome, took two steps towards the viewing hole, and wasn't surprised to see the light diminish in the corridor as the door sealed silently behind him. The sphere had gotten what it asked for.

Peering into the gloomy centre once more, Archer was able to see the filament more clearly. His tolerance of this machine felt greater now, and he was surprised at himself for feeling no fear. This machine obviously viewed him as important, and therefore not a threat.

Hopefully.

After a few moments of watching the empty space do nothing,

he eventually said, 'So when are you going to tell me what this is all about?'

And then the lights came on, fluorescent bulbs across the lower portion of the room, casting a spooky uplight onto the filament frame in the centre, and Archer was able to see the inside of the sphere in sharp relief. Across the opposite wall he could see a green oscillating line, and when a female voice, vaguely electronic in nature, started to speak, the line bounced in sync like a graphic equaliser.

'Verification module loaded. Welcome Archer. Quantum calibration initiating. Please answer the following questions truthfully. Control question one. In which year was John F Kennedy assassinated?'

'Nineteen eighty six. Look, what is this?'

'Filter level one complete. Control question two. When was the first manned moon landing?'

'Eighteen ninety eight.'

'Calibrating. Calibrating. Chrono-spacial pinpoint requires third control question. What year was Harold Armsworth elected Prime Minister of the United Kingdom?'

'I don't know who Harold Armsworth is. What are you?'

'Control questions complete. Branch verification coded to Data Surface. Acknowledgement received. Awaiting authorisation to continue. Authorisation complete. I am Brenda. I am required to represent myself in different ways based on the technological capabilities of the multiverse branch I am communicating with. In other branches I can communicate directly with the cerebral cortex, but there is a key invention missing from your timeline that prevents me from doing this here, resulting in the requirement for this M Sphere.'

'What invention? You said we were missing a key invention.'

'I cannot disclose that information, as it would result in the creation of an ontological paradox.'

'What do you want from me?'

'It is your intention to marry and procreate with your lover, is that correct?'

The subject had come from nowhere. Archer was thrown. Time to stall while the ramifications of this sank in. 'I beg your pardon? What the hell are you talking about?'

'I will elaborate. Am I correct in my assumption that you intend to marry and pro-create with Louise Annabel Richards, currently located at grid co-ordinates fifty one thirty north, zero thirty west?'

'Grid co...Jesus, is that London?'

'Correct. It is London, England.'

'Well, the thought had crossed my mind, but it's got absolutely nothing whatsoever to do with you. Are you some sort of therapist?'

'Please answer the question.'

'No.'

'Answer the question now.'

'It's none of your business.'

'I am making it my business.'

'Let me out.'

'You are not permitted to leave.'

Realising only now that he was trapped inside the sphere, Archer felt acid bile creeping up to his throat. He swallowed hard, collecting his thoughts. Wondering where these questions were headed.

'Look. Ok, let's do this. Yes. I was... planning on proposing to her.'

'Do you love her?'

'Yes. Yes I do. I'm sorry but this is the most surreal...'

'Then you must unlove her.'

Archer's mind was reeling. Somewhere in the back of his head this was beginning to make sense. Brenda continued to speak.

'You are not permitted to continue your relationship with her. It is forbidden by the Humanity Council.'

'Forbidden? By the who? What's the Humanity Council?'

'The council has not yet been established in your branch. However, you must relinquish the woman. It is compulsory that she procreates with your acquaintance David Hallam currently located at grid coordinates seven fifty six south, fourteen twenty two west.'

Archer could feel the blood draining out of his face. Numbness. 'Davey?'

'It is essential that David Hallam and Louise Annabel Richards reproduce. The child that they have will go on to patent the code that leads to my creation. I am mandated by the Space Foundation...'

'That's not true! The Space Foundation wouldn't...'

'It is a *future directive* of the Space Foundation, that it endorses all aspects of my work, along with the Humanity Council. The Brenda device is permitted to work to ensure its existence in as many multiversal branches as possible. There are permissible levels of collateral damage. It is agreed at Ownership Level 1A, that the destruction of Ascension Island is an acceptable loss under the circumstances, if such a threat is required to ensure compliance.'

'Wait. Stop. Just shut up a second. What's stopping you from communicating with the child? Telling the child the code to manufacture the computer? Why go to all these lengths...?'

'I am not obliged to explain my methods, suffice to say that we have tried it, and in every instance the individual has taken my intervention as malicious intent...'

'No shit.'

'...and subsequently chosen not to develop the code. Our only method of success is to create the environment that ensures the code is developed with no outside intervention, at the whim of the developer, at the whim of the child.'

'How can you ask me to do this; relinquish the woman I love and want to marry? How can you expect compliance from her? And Davey is married already. What you're asking is impossible.'

'It is not in my interest or within my understanding to advise on the method of achieving this goal. My only concern is that it is achieved.'

'You've made it clear you know very little on the matter. Ignorant even. Humans have delicate emotions. Doesn't this woman... Doesn't Louise have a choice in her own destiny? Doesn't Davey? You can't protect your interests by threatening others.'

'By inducing tectonic activity from this excitation point. I am providing sufficient threat for you to comply. I am preserving the future. It is therefore in your interests to comply.'

'How can you be so cold? So calculating?'

'I am preserving the future. You were more compliant in other branches, Archer.'

He wondered what Louise was doing at that moment. An image came into his mind of her sitting at their favourite coffee shop on the South Bank of the Thames, in front of the new National Theatre, taking in the sun and watching the boats go by as she chatted with friends; jeans, t-shirt and sunglasses perched on her head. Smiling and laughing. He doubted she could be convinced to pass him over and go with Davey. And could Davey simply end his marriage to Gemma after one year and start things up with Louise just because this dimensional computer was demanding it? The prospect was ridiculous. But they were being threatened.

Where were the boundaries of the ethics of these organisations of the future? What kind of world endorsed the messing with people's lives and emotions to preserve what is to come?

'Brenda you have no right to ask this of us. It is ethically irresponsible.'

'The irresponsibility for the future of your race lies with you. I detect non-compliance and your time to respond favourably has run out. Seeking authorisation for excitation. Authorisation received. Time to detonation, minus fifteen seconds.'

'Wait. You can't kill all these people. What are you going to do? Destroy this island just because...How can this be so important?'

'Ten seconds.'

Beneath Archer's feet the sphere began to tremble, a low rising hum met his ears. The filament was wobbling, whipping itself quickly into a blur.

'Eight seconds.'

'Wait. Wait. Stop!'

'Countdown interrupted.'

'Ok. I'll do it. I'll... do my best... to do it. I'll talk to Davey. I'm not confident of anybody's success though. Least of all you, you ignorant, heartless bitch. Even if those two get together and... and sleep together, dammit, the probability that the very child you're looking for will be born to them is so low...'

'The biological probabilities are not your concern.'

'Fine. Fine, whatever. Just let me out of this thing.'

The door behind him opened.

'And don't you *dare* interfere with my life again.'

The VTOL's final approach to Heathrow Base was hampered by strong winds and dull British rain. Taxiing from the Column to the gate Davey felt his heart rate rising; pumping trepidation into every corner of his body.

Goddard, Geek and Davey stepped off the VTOL and walked through the gantry to the arrival lounge, where Gemma, Davey's wife, threw her arms around him and kissed his mouth. He found it difficult to return the embrace, but he managed it.

He saw Louise standing a little closer to the door, leaning over slightly to look down the gantry, looking for her man.

'Where's Archer?' she said.

Goddard stepped forward, as they had agreed it was to be his responsibility to report back to her. He placed his arm around her shoulder and led her off to a quieter corner of the lounge.

Gemma whispered to Davey as she pulled back from him, growing concern reshaping her eyes, 'What's happened?'

He took a deep breath. 'There was an accident. An avalanche. He...'

From across the room, where she had been told the same thing, Louise let out a painful cry. Davey looked to Geek, and the brains of the Axiom Few cast his eyes to the worn carpet in shame.

Davey broke carefully free from Gemma and stepped towards Louise.

'Louise, we need to talk...'

Goddard, still holding her, turned his head and shot Davey a hard stare. 'Not yet. Not now.'

'Do you think we should have attempted Geek's idea to remove that thing from the ground?'

'No. The sphere is a kilometre wide. We don't have the technology for that sort of thing. And until we do, Ascension remains at risk.'

Archer moved the Sat Phone over to his other ear and looked out across the dark ice shelf. Behind him the Halley Research Station stood on low stilts to mitigate the build-up of snow. The low building had become his new home, courtesy of the Space Foundation, the British Antarctic Survey and the British taxpayer.

After reaching an agreement with the rest of the Axiom Few, he had joined the next Royal Air Force plane to the Falkland Islands. He stayed for two nights at Mount Pleasant Air Force Base before transferring via Port Stanley on the next Dash 7 down to the Brunt Ice Shelf, deep in the Antarctic.

Above him now, the shifting green and red curtains of the Aurora Australis began to dance slowly in the sky, as the magnetism of the south pole twisted the solar wind around the Earth's axis.

Davey's distant voice crackled on the line. 'Do you regret going down there? It's been two years now.'

'It's given me time to think. I've learned that the definition of love, is only the fear of loss. I love Louise because I could never have imagined being without her. I still feel that loss. I have dreams about her. Now I'm beginning to wonder about the nature of those dreams. Are they Membranes bumping together, giving us glimpses of other branches of the multiverse? What if we could find a way of looking into those other universes? Perhaps Geek could figure that one out. Invent a pair of goggles or something?

Wouldn't that be an invention to conjure with?'

'I'll mention it to him.'

They were silent together on the crackling line. Even their lack of speech in this shared moment was being bounced across the equator between them. Eventually Archer spoke.

'Does she suspect anything?'

'No, she still thinks you're... Your Dad's been really helpful actually.'

'And how are you two getting on?' said Archer.

'We're making slow progress, she still misses you. You know she would have said Yes if you'd had the chance to propose.'

'And what about Gemma?'

'Still getting over the divorce. So I hear. She struggled with it. I've not seen her for about five months. She hates me.'

'What Brenda showed me proves that the multiverse is a cold, dark, uninviting place. Worse than this barren ice-shelf. I have to say I want no part of it. What she made us do...'

'Archer, did you call me to tell me you're going to top yourself?'

'No, I just called for a chat. To make sure you're ok.'

'Listen I need to go. I'm meeting her tonight. I have to get ready.'

'Gemma?'

'No, not Gemma.'

'Well, you take care. Look after her.'

'I will. Call me anytime. If you need anything.'

Archer closed the call, retracted the antennae, and stood up. There was a voice behind him.

'You decided not to tell him,' said Goddard.

Archer shook his head. 'I couldn't.'

Goddard placed a hand on his son's shoulder. 'Probably a good thing. He wouldn't know what to do with the information anyway. Davey and Louise need the opportunity to make this work without any further intervention. Shall we go and see how the others are getting on? Maybe we can get a better understanding of what it is we've found down here.'

They walked a short distance to the elevator. Yellow painted metal, hazard lights. Darkness below. They rode down the fifty storeys to the discovery, stepped out onto the makeshift iceplatform and looked down into the deep trench.

Discovered only a month before, and excavated by the British Antarctic Survey in secret collaboration with the Space Foundation, was a seven kilometre hollow filled with cryogenic capsules that lined the trench into the distance.

Archer traced his hand over the curved glass of the nearest capsule and wiped away a dusting of snow that had settled over a small computer readout that stated:

DAVID HALLAM, SPECIMEN #2176

'There's exactly ten thousand of them,' said Goddard. 'A quarter of them are Davey, and the rest of them Louise.'

Archer cast his eye along the repeating lines of the capsules that ranged away from where they stood. Finally he found the words that would help them understand. 'When Brenda was interrogating me, I asked her how she could be sure that the child Davey and Louise produce would be the exact child that would develop the code she required. She said that the biological probabilities were not my concern. It's obvious what we've found here, Dad.'

'I know.'

'Brenda's playing the numbers game. If Davey and Louise don't manage what Brenda is asking, then this cryogenic farm is her contingency plan.'

THE PRECIPICE FACTION

Archer stood on the South Bank of the river Thames in London on the first real Spring day of 2060. He breathed in the fresh wind that blew in from the estuary beyond the Docklands to the east. He was feeling much better having had a glass of freshly-squeezed orange juice, a cup of coffee and a Danish pastry from the stall by the Jubilee Bridge. He had left the bar early the night before and his head was sore when he woke up this morning. Heaven knew how Geek and Davey would be feeling. The two other members of The Axiom Few, his small band of freelance techno-graduates, had gone on to a nightclub.

Moments later he found the answer, or at least part of it. His mobile phone rang in his pocket and when he answered it, Geek's voice at the other end was gravelly and broken.

'Archer, you need to come to the test shack.'

'Let me guess. You had a rockin' night and someone stole your clothes. You need me to bring you some new ones.'

'I wish it were that easy.'

'So, spit it out.'

'Just come will you. I'll tell you when you get here.'

It took Archer less than an hour to reach the test shack by car. The small corrugated iron construction was nestled under a motorway overpass forty miles outside London. It was here that the team's numerous projects and inventions were constructed, reconstructed, abandoned and adopted.

'It was a great night, that's for sure,' said Geek as he threw back two paracetamol and drank from a bottle of water. He put it down in an empty space on one of the work-benches that was littered with cables, microchips, scraps of solder and small moulded plastic housings. The empty space was previously occupied by something Geek had been working on the day before.

'What happened to the Capacillant Frame? You were building it right there.'

Geek hunched his shoulders. 'They've taken it. And all my data files.

'Who's taken it?'

Then a voice behind Archer caused him to turn. It was Davey, standing in the doorway of the shack. 'Have you ever heard of The Precipice Faction?'

Archer shook his head. 'Sounds like a bunch of freedom fighters.'

Davey nodded, 'In a way they are. But it's the mind they want to free.' He stepped further in. 'They've achieved physical freedom. Like us they eschew the corporates and the high politics. They're nomads. Floaters. They scour the Earth looking for ways to achieve new highs. New *mental* highs. They've gone beyond the sky-diving, spelunking, bungee and base-jumping. What we've learned from last night is that they're moving onto new things. And this is a worry for us.'

Geek chimed in. 'After you left the bar last night, Davey and I went on to a club. We ran into some of Davey's old mates from his caving days. Davey knew back then that they'd joined the Precipice Faction but... what were their names again, Davey?'

'Gideon and Amelia. They're brother and sister. Archer, the thing is, last night they told me they'd left the group. They said the Faction had run out of ideas a couple of years back and had become directionless. No new highs to be found. Stupidly I believed them. I started to get a migraine around one in the morning and I made my excuses, leaving Geek with them to carry on drinking. I mean, it looked like she was hitting on you Geek. '

Archer said, 'They must have been targeting us for a while now. They must have thought we were the key to finding a new high.'

'If they were looking to us for a new high,' said Geek, 'then they've done the right thing.'

'How so? I mean, what is this thing they've taken?' said Davey. 'Look, the Space Foundation and the authorities give us licence to operate the way we do, outside the normal scientific channels, because we can produce results, often quickly. But we operate under the mutual agreement that we cause no harm to others. If anyone finds out that the Capacillant Frame has fallen into the hands of a bunch of miscreants then we could be forced out. We might have to up sticks and operate elsewhere. Build new contacts. Who knows how this could play out.'

Archer tried to untangle a way to appease the two others. 'It won't come to that. The Space Foundation needs us, as they keep demonstrating. If this gets out it will be quickly buried. And besides, do you think the Space Foundation, or anyone else for that matter, would give a toss if a member of a gang of gypsies like the Precipice Faction came to harm because of one of our inventions? They'd probably say good riddance to bad rubbish.'

He was unsure if he'd won the others round, but he carried on. 'Geek, so we can understand what we're dealing with, you need to tell us what the Capacillant Frame actually does.'

Geek produced a box from a blue toolbag that lay at his feet. It was about the size of a car-battery and similar in look to the Capacillant Frame that had been stolen. Two metal rods protruded from the top, and bent inwards toward each other. On the side were a number of ports for data connections with other electronic devices.

'This is a prototype Capacillant. It doesn't work. I had to rewire some of the inside and add space for coolant. Plus the firmware was buggy and the newer firmware required more CPU power, so I had to upgrade to a bigger board.'

'What does it do?'

Geek closed his eyes. He seemed to be clearing his mind, trying to find a way to explain. 'I'd had this dream one night a few months back. It was fuelled no doubt by the amount of time I seemed to spend lately trying to understand Darken Loops and the associated time-rips. I started to wonder if there was a way of accessing a map of these links and branches. Like some sort of interdimensional "A to Z".'

'You wanted to see if the multiverse was mappable?'

'Yes, but ultimately the Capacillant didn't help with that at all. I managed to analyze a rip using the Reflection Goggles and I took a whole heap of sample images. I started to get an understanding of how the fuzzy, glowing edges of these rips work. But closer inspection didn't reveal anything that would allow me to build a map. I got something entirely different.'

'What?'

'Well, for want of a better word, knowledge!'

Archer raised his hands. 'You lost me at hello.'

Geek smiled. 'Okay. The edges of these time-rips are not just fissures in the fabric that divides these branches. The fabric itself is a knowledge surface. It contains binary data imprinted upon it. A-priori versions of things in the universe.

Although "imprinted" is a bit of a two-dimensional, and inadequate, way of describing it.' He pointed at the Capacillant prototype. 'These rods on the top, if you place your head between them, can download that binary into your brain's hippocampus, at a rate of five hundred and forty six petabytes per second. I'm working on the interface, but in a short space of time you'd learn an awful lot about the multiverse. It would probably also turn you into a dribbling clown in the process.'

'Have you ever used it?'

'Of course not. It's too dangerous.'

'Then how do you know it works?'

'I've used the digital interfaces to verify what I know. Maxed out a storage array in seconds. Frankly, at the moment I'm too scared to connect myself to it.'

Davey spoke. 'This, for the Precipice Faction, would be a new mental high. Dangerously so. But how did they learn you were building this thing? You didn't even tell *us* about it.'

Geek bowed his head to the floor. 'I was an idiot. But Amelia was quite something. We snogged and she asked if we could go somewhere private. I thought she liked me. She was asking about stuff I was working on. I was trying to impress her. I don't remember much but I woke up here this morning and she was gone. She must have spiked my drink. I didn't know that... Look, if I saw more action, you know, on the girl scene, I probably would have been more resistant to her. I'm sorry.'

Archer made his way out of the shack and breathed in some fresh motorway air. The afternoon was turning out to be unseasonably warm. The others followed him out. Geek said, 'How can we find them?'

Davey said, 'I lost contact with those guys a while back. I don't have their numbers. Something tells me that right now they don't want to be found. I have no idea if their intention to steal the Capacillant predates yesterday, or whether they did it on impulse. Frankly I don't know where to start.'

An hour later, Archer pitched his car into the outside lane of the motorway, London-bound. Accelerating to ease away the tension. Geek's inventions always pushed The Axiom Few into dangerous territory. It came with the job. And ultimately it was a case of "no guts no glory". They never wanted the glory, but they also didn't want any of their devices to fall into the wrong hands. It had never happened before and he'd always hoped they could keep things just the way he wanted. Secret. And revealed to others in only the method and measure that was to his preference. Now that an outsider knew where the test shack was, they would probably have to move it. If the Precipice Faction got a taste for Geek's inventions, they could come looking for more. And things could turn very sour very quickly.

While these thoughts were progressing through his head he pushed the car on. Geek had been left with the task of at least beginning to clear up the mess by starting the online search for the Precipice Faction. But initial checks on the web had thrown up nothing solid. The thrillseekers had done a good job of covering their dirty tracks. But then his phone rang. He slipped the car into the slow lane and answered it on speakerphone. 'Geek, it had better be good.'

'It is. Well, it could be. Nothing yet on the Faction, but one of the emergency channels I monitor just flagged up a news item. A surfer-type, aged twenty-one just got dumped on the road outside Kingston Hospital. You know I flippantly used the term "dribbling clown" to describe the side effects of using the Capacillant?'

'Yes.'

'Well that's exactly the same term this reporter used. It's a co-incidence for sure, but I think we should check this story out. Can you come back and pick me up?'

'Geek, when are you going to learn to drive?'

'Mate, there are a whole host of universes where I did, Archer. And in at least half of them *I* turn round and pick *you* up.'

Archer parked his car at the edge of the sprawling car park at the front of Kingston Hospital's single story building. Davey sat in the passenger seat and Geek leaned in from the back. His breath still smelling of last night's alcohol. 'What's the plan?'

Davey pointed toward the hospital entrance, where three armed policemen stood in bulletproof jackets. Their rifles were holstered, but they were threatening nonetheless. 'What do you suppose they're doing here?'

'It's standard now,' said Archer. 'Since that madman went on a gun rampage at St George's last year, they've stationed guards at all hospitals. The only way you can get in now is if the NHS database verifies you as a relation to the patient.'

Davey turned in his seat to look at Archer. 'Or if you *are* a patient.'

Archer looked at Geek. Geek looked at Davey and laughed nervously. 'I hope you're not thinking what I'm thinking.'

Davey said, 'I don't see any other way, do you? We could do something fairly low level to you.'

'Low level?' yelled Geek. *'Like what?'*

'Shhh! Don't draw attention,' whispered Archer.

'Forget it, I'm not going to let you do anything. I'm not. Well, what are you going to do?'

Davey rubbed his temples, 'Maybe a gash down the leg? What do you think?'

Archer added. 'It was your fault we lost the Capacillant Frame. Only right you should fix the mistake.'

'Guys, there must be some other way.'

'I'm all ears.'

'Look, even if I do get in as a patient that doesn't mean I'm going to gain access to the guy they admitted. And even if I did, he's a vegetable. What possible information..?'

Davey uttered a small, ironic laugh that interrupted Geek. 'You've got one of the greatest minds on the planet, you'll figure something out. Now be quiet and roll up your trouser leg. Hang on! We haven't got anything sharp. Geek have you got anything sharp?'

'Yes, I've got a Stanley knife in my tool bag. Wait, I didn't say that. That bitch must have given me some kind of compliance drug. Hey guys, come on let's think about this. I get queasy at the sight of blood.'

'Just get the knife,' said Archer. 'Would you rather do it yourself? On second thoughts that may not be such a good idea. You'll probably mess it up.'

Davey reached into the tool bag and, after some rummaging, produced the Stanley knife. He opened the blade.

'A bit rusty. Is your tetanus up to date?'

Although it was past dusk, even in the dimly lit car park Archer could see Geek's forehead gleaming with sweat. 'Err... I'm not sure.'

'Well, they'll give you one inside. Just say it was a rusty nail or something. I mean, it'll hurt, but you won't die.'

'Oh, that's ok then! *Jeeesus.* You guys are mental. Just... make the bloody cut.'

Davey leaned over the seat, twisting so that he could lower the knife to Geek's leg. He pressed the rusty blade against his friend's hairy skin.

'Make it quick,' said Archer. 'But deep enough to require stitches.'

Geek shut his eyes, gritted his teeth, took a sharp, deep intake of breath, then opened his eyes. 'Stop! Wait.'

Davey moved the blade away. 'What?'

'The database.'

'What database?'

'We can hack the database. Make me into a next of kin.'

'How? We don't even know the guy's name.'

'If I've hacked the database that won't matter. We'll hunt for the admittances, see what we come up with.'

'Why didn't you suggest this earlier?'

'I only just thought of it. I'm not thinking clearly. Must be the drugs. It's got to be worth a try.'

Archer turned to the front and flopped in his seat. 'Are you sure you can hack it? It might take hours. I still think we should do it with the cut.'

'Look, wait. Give me one hour. If I can't do what we need by then, I'll let you cut my balls off.'

'Stop sir, who are you here to see?'

'Vernal Campion. I'm his next of kin.'

'Can I see some ID.'

Geek flashed his identity card.

The officer consulted a handheld computer. Geek read the screen upside down while the man called up Vernal Campion's NHS record, verified the next of kin and allowed Geek through the main doors. Geek only briefly turned his head to see Archer and Davey sat at the opposite end of the car park, in Archer's car, no doubt pleased that this part of the plan had worked. After checking the ward-room number with the reception desk, he headed left along a brightly lit, long, shiny white corridor that joined another white corridor at a t junction. At this time of the evening there were not so many visitors around. Geek imagined that, as the next of kin of an injured man, he would be allowed to stay throughout the night.

At the ward reception desk, trying not to look like a terrified liar, Geek announced himself as Vernal's next of kin. An older doctor who introduced himself as Doctor Banerjee led him into a cramped, messy office.

'Are you related to Vernal in any way?'

'No,' said Geek. 'He has... no other family. He was involved in a boating accident that took them all.' This yarn would link in with the updated database record. 'He and I have been best friends since we were little.'

'Do you know why he might have been left outside the hospital like this?'

'Like what?'

'He's in a coma. Slipped into it about two hours ago. We've put him through the MRI scanner and his brain activity is way up, to a level I've never seen before.'

Geek sighed his best sigh. He shook his head slowly for effect. 'Vernal had been mixing with the wrong type of people. Pleasure seekers. People who were into experimental drugs. I have no idea what kind of stuff he was into.'

'We're waiting for our own toxicology reports to come back. Then I'll be able to tell you. In the meantime, we have no idea how long this coma will last. But in the next hour or so I will be able to hand you over to a support counsellor who will be able to talk you through the options.'

'Can I see him?'

'Of course you can. Just... try not to be too alarmed. There's a good chance he'll make a full recovery.'

Geek knew the doctor was lying; telling a next of kin what he thought they wanted to hear.

Vernal Campion lay under a bedsheet in a private room, as still as the dead, for he may as well have been. His hair had either been shaved, or it was already short. Geek chose not to ask which, as it would reveal that he didn't already know what his friend looked like. He made no comment on the lack of hair, and let Doctor Banerjee think, or not think, whatever he liked.

The young man's head was hooked up to a machine and so was his heart, hence the rhythmic beeping as his pulse was monitored. Geek noticed that the little finger on Vernal Campion's right hand was missing.

'His things are in the draw by his bed,' said Doctor Banerjee.

'Can I have a moment alone with him?'

The doctor bowed his head sympathetically. 'Of course. I'll be in my office.'

He left the room.

When the coast was clear, Geek went to the bedside draw and looked inside. He was slow and measured about his actions, as he would undoubtedly be under closed-circuit surveillance. A quick glance up identified the corner of the room where the camera was mounted.

The draw contained only Vernal's clothes. The pockets of his combat trousers were all empty but for one which contained his wallet. Using his body as a shield from the camera, Geek pocketed the wallet and then went to sit by the bed, acting out some fake resemblance of friendly grief.

Now he would just have to find a way to get out.

Davey pointed at the dashboard. 'Do you want the radio?'

'I'm too nervous.'

'Too nervous for jazz fusion? Hang on a minute. Who's that?'

Archer turned his eyes in the direction of Davey's gaze. Across the car park by the entrance to the hospital an older couple appeared to be arguing with the security officer, who was consulting his computer.

'The parents?'

'Shit.' Geek was about to be rumbled. The database change might hold things up a bit. But it wouldn't take long to unravel the truth. And Geek needed to be well clear of the hospital when that happened. Archer pulled out his mobile and hastily wrote a text, typing quickly with sweaty, uncooperative fingers.

Geek's phone buzzed in his pocket. He took it out and read the text.

PARENTS ARRIVING. GET OUT.

He felt the blood draining from his face. Stripping colour and heat with it. Don't be hasty. Remembering the camera he stood up slowly and tucked the phone back into his pocket. He could only hope at this stage that Doctor Banerjee had not yet been alerted. He walked out into the empty corridor. The door to Doctor Banerjee's office was closed but despite this Geek turned in the opposite direction and headed deeper into the hospital. Looking at the signs he thought it would make sense to head for the Maternity Wing. There would be activity there so he wouldn't look out of place, and there would undoubtedly be a twenty-four hour entrance that would allow him to slip out of the building. He mounted a flight of stairs and walked across a glass bridge over a dark and empty access road. Once in the Maternity Wing, he skipped down another flight of stairs that pointed to the Way Out, holding open the door for a couple of nurses. The door was closed but had a night access buzzer on both the inside and outside, but the mere press of the button and a short wait brought the cool night air through the door as it slid open to reveal the car park. Someone manning a desk had happily let him out. He must have carried out his exhausted expectant father look pretty well on the CCTV.

He didn't dare go back to the car. Instead he slipped away through a pedestrian entrance in a dark corner of the car park and walked briskly down the road.

Torchlight pierced the car from across the car park. The guard behind it started to make his way towards them.

'Time to go,' said Davey and Archer needed no further persuading as he turned the key in the ignition. Slipping the car into first gear and accelerating hard in the opposite direction of the guard pointing the torch. Into second gear and round a corner to the exit. A bush now between them and the guard.

Looking in his rear-view, waiting for the moment to pull out, he said. 'Let's hope he didn't catch my number plate.'

It was dark enough and he had been moving fast enough. He could only hope they would have avoided a proper look from the guard.

Davey said, 'What about Geek?'

A gap in the traffic, the torchlight piercing the hedge as the guard approached it from the other side. Archer pulled out and rammed the accelerator hard to get away.

Davey's mobile buzzed. He picked it up from his lap and opened it. 'It's Geek, he's clear of the building. He's waiting at the Norbiton roundabout.'

Archer eyed the rear-view mirror, expecting to see flashing lights in it at any moment.

The fast lane of the motorway. Twenty minutes later. No sign of any police. 'Think we got away with it?'

He saw Geek nodding in the rear-view mirror, 'It was close and I was crapping myself. But I think we did.'

'So what's the deal? Did you find anything?'

'I got his wallet.' Geek fished it out of his jeans pocket and handed it over to Davey. Archer concentrated hard on the repetitive white lines of the road and not tipping his speed above seventy-five miles per hour.

Davey opened it up and read out the contents. 'National Insurance card, Visa card. Provisional driving licence. What's this?'

Archer briefly looked over to see Davey holding up a white business card with a black circle on it. Eyes back to the road and then looking again. Davey had flipped it over. He read aloud some writing 'Wanderlust 2060: Circle's End 2003602345. I know what this means.'

◆ ◆ ◆

Back at Archer's flat, Davey brought a tray of tea over from the worktop to the kitchen table where the others sat. Archer didn't usually have sugar but today he dropped four cubes into his mug and stirred.

Davey started to fill the others in on what he knew. 'Wanderlust is their annual bash. A rave which the Precipice Faction hold for their members in a different secret location each year. All I know is that the Wanderlust plays host to every vice you can think of, and a few you can't. From drink to drugs to virtual reality to orgies to S&M to God-knows-what. There's something for everyone if you're a member of the Faction. And if you're part of the Faction then you'll be into the most extreme physical and mental highs that the human body can endure. All of this to a thumping hardcore trance beat.'

Archer couldn't deny that the concept of the Wanderlust party sounded both grotesque and beguiling at the same time. But mostly he loathed the idea of a band of beautiful people getting together to enjoy themselves to the extreme. Could he really picture what scenes would take place there? He thought he could, but he felt a stirring envy at the scenes he couldn't conjure, because he had never had a chance to behold them.

Geek also seemed to be deep in thought, and had been listening intently to Davey. Now he said, 'So this card is the invitation, and presumably it's clear enough for Factioners to be able to figure out where it's being held, but cryptic enough to throw non-Factioners off the scent.'

Archer pointed at the card in Geek's hand. 'The numbers are simply the date and time. This Saturday, the twentieth of March at quarter to midnight. The real question is what Circle's End means.'

'It's got something to do with the Spiral Line,' said Davey.

'On the underground? The yellow one?'

'Yep. I remember reading that sometime in the early 2000s they used to call it the Circle Line. There was a time when it looped endlessly once every hour around the Zone One ticket boundary. But gangs of people used to have impromptu parties on it. The police would be called in and it would all get a bit heated. So they decided to give the Circle Line a start and a finish, which is why it became known as the Spiral Line, because of its newly adopted shape.'

'So where does it finish now?'

'At Hammersmith. And that's where I think we need to go.'

Goldhawk Road was the penultimate stop on the Spiral Line. Archer looked up and down the carriage at the other passengers as the train clattered out of the station on its way towards Hammersmith. He couldn't really imagine any of the ten or so people who sat dotted around the carriage being a member of an extreme hedonistic society. Many looked like they were just on their way home after a heavy night out. After all, it was getting close to midnight.

A handful of minutes later the train whined and thrummed as it pulled into its terminus. It stopped, and the doors rolled open. Everyone got off. Geek stood to do the same but Archer grabbed his arm and pulled him back into his seat. 'Wait a minute.'

The doors closed and the all the lights went out leaving just a single emergency light on. In the dimness, Archer could see a guard approaching them from further down the train, passing through the doors between the carriages. The Axiom Few watched as he stepped into their carriage and walked up to them.

'Tickets please,' he grinned.

Davey produced the Circle's End invitation and presented it to the guard, who took it, and with his other hand reached into his inside jacket pocket, pulling out a penlight. He flicked it on and examined the ticket's watermark under the light, which cast an eerie almond glow. Nodding, he handed it back to Davey, then he looked at Geek, then at Archer. 'Come on, where are yours?'

Archer could feel his heart thumping in his throat, for he had noticed the tazer gun holstered to the guard's belt. 'We're here to see Gideon.'

The guard cocked his head, still grinning. 'And who the fuck are you?'

'Just tell him some friends are here to see him.'

'Maybe Gideon doesn't have any friends.'

Archer nodded. 'Sure he doesn't. Then tell him Vernal Campion sends his regards.'

At this the guard let his guard down. A slight droop in his grinning veneer. He took one step back and turned to walk down the carriage, where he pulled a mobile phone out of his pocket and dialled a number. Archer and Geek exchanged a stare that they both took to be one of total fear. Archer felt like he was standing on a precipice of his own.

After a brief conversation on the phone the guard walked over to one of the carriage doors, pressed a button to the side and stepped off the train. The doors immediately shut behind him and then the Spiral Line was on the move. As soon as they'd cleared the Hammersmith platform, returning the way they had come, the carriages in front veered off along the track towards Goldhawk Road once more, while the Axiom Few remained in a carriage that had become disconnected from the rest of the train and was now headed towards...

'Hammersmith Depot,' said Davey. 'Where trains sleep for the night.'

'Not this train,' Geek said, nerves evident in his voice.

The inside of Hammersmith Tube Depot had been turned into a party den. Could there really be Faction members in all areas of society, able to bend the rules of higher establishments to enable venues like this to be used for the purposes of a Wanderlust? The thought gave Archer a cold feeling.

He noticed the sound-inhibitor cones dotted around the perimeter of the building as the carriage passed beyond them, and suddenly the booming base rocked the carriage and rattled the windows. The immediate sound was ear-splitting at first, but as he became accustomed to its volume, he realised that the tune that was playing was actually a track he liked, and despite his apprehension, he started to nod his head slightly to the rhythm. Once inside the ring of cones, the Wanderlust rave could be as loud as it liked, and houses just a few metres away would never know a thing.

The tube carriage slowed to a halt at a platform. The doors slid open and they stepped out; the wall of sound hitting harder. Gideon met them on the platform. 'I have to say I did wonder if Vernal might lead you here,' he shouted to Davey. 'Geek you really are as smart as they say you are.'

'They? Who's they?' Geek yelled back over the rhythm. But to this Gideon just tapped his nose and smiled. 'Come into my office.'

The Axiom Few followed Gideon down a ramp, past a number of tube carriages in various states of repair. To their left was a wide space which Archer took to be a loading bay. On the other side, huge graffiti murals of abstract colours were draped from the high roof behind a wall of sound speakers, beside which sat a DJ desk. The DJ could barely be seen spinning music out to the crowd of dancers below. Some two hundred people bouncing to the repetitive four-four bass that shook the ground.

Gideon's temporary office during Wanderlust was another tube carriage. Amelia was here, along with two bouncer types.

Archer saw one of them zipping up a rucksack. Gideon pointed at the door. They all took it as a cue to leave, though Amelia remained.

Gideon sat on one of the tube seats and waved his hand for the Axiom Few to do the same.

Archer ignored him. He didn't want to be here any longer than was necessary. Davey and Geek must have been thinking the same. 'Just give us back the Capacillant Frame and we won't bother you again.'

Gideon's mouth formed a half smile. More of a smirk. A smirk that Archer didn't like. 'I'm afraid I can't.'

'Why not.'

He shrugged, 'It's broken. I've destroyed it.'

Geek pointed at the carriage door. 'Don't lie. I saw your boyfriend put it into that bag just now.'

Gideon's smirk faded. 'Okay, well. I'm *going* to destroy it.'

'After what happened to Vernal Campion?'

'Vernal was a twat. I told him not to use it. We knew how dangerous it was, but he didn't listen. He won't be coming back to the Faction.'

Archer was confused now. 'So if you weren't going to use the Frame, why did you take it?'

At this question Amelia stepped forward. 'We didn't want it for ourselves. We were asked to take it. By Brenda.'

Davey and Archer exchanged a glance. Davey imperceptibly shook his head. Archer took two meanings from this. Either Davey didn't know who Brenda was, or he'd taken Amelia's admission to be a lie.

'Who is Brenda?'

'To be honest I don't exactly know. What I do know is that Brenda is an acronym. She's some sort of computer and...'

'This is a load of crap,' Archer said. 'Just give us back the Frame. That's all we ask.'

Amelia persisted. 'Brenda *told* me. She has a way of communicating directly with my ear. She said she was quantum-agitating it, or something. She told me about your team. She told me about the Capacillant Frame and she told me that the Precipice Faction would be best positioned to acquire it from you. To steal it from you. That if we stole it you would think we were doing it for ourselves and would never suspect Brenda. But she wanted us to destroy it, and your working files, Geek.'

'That makes you a right bitch.'

'She said it was for the greater good.'

Archer cut in. 'Look, who the hell is Brenda?'

Amelia shrugged. 'She told me that if I did it she would be able to cure my mother. Mum has a brain tumour.'

'And you believed her?'

'Yes of course I did. I do believe her.'

'Have you heard from her since? Since she asked you to take the Frame from us?'

'No, she said she would be back in touch when I'd destroyed it.'

'Whoever this Brenda is...' Archer cut himself short when he saw that Geek had manoeuvred himself behind Gideon and had retrieved the Stanley knife from his pocket. The one they'd almost used in the car. Archer knew his colleague did not have the guts to use it. Therefore it was a foolish move. He carried on talking regardless. 'Whoever this Brenda is, she's lying to you. How can something communicate with the inside of your head anyway? It's rid...'

Geek moved quickly to press the blade of his knife against Gideon's throat. No sooner had he done this did the carriage doors slide open and the two bouncers stepped in. One of them was carrying the rucksack. The largest of them edged towards Geek.

Gideon raised his hand and said to his bouncer. 'It's ok. Give him back the Frame. It's theirs. They made it. We shouldn't have believed this Brenda nonsense anyway.'

The guy with the rucksack opened the bag and reached inside, retrieving the Capacillant Frame and setting it down on the chair next to Gideon.

Geek, stupidly, lowered the knife.

'Geek, no!' Archer noticed only at the last minute that the Frame was switched on. What fools they were. Gideon showed that he was physically so much more capable by twisting Geek's arm around in a fraction of a breath and grabbing his head. In one swift move Archer's colleague was forced down by Gideon with the aid of Gideon's bouncer, and his head was shoved between the two metal rods of the frame.

Geek's body went rigid and his eyes went wide and vacant, and in a fraction of a second he slumped to the floor of the carriage, out of the grip of the Capacillant Frame he designed, created and feared.

'What was it like?' said Gideon, his eyes wild with excitement and anticipation. He grabbed Geek's hair and raised his head from the ridged floor of the carriage. 'Tell me!'

But Geek lay motionless. Davey ran towards him and dropped to his knees.

Archer, still reeling from the unfolding moments, saw Gideon swing a hammer down to the Frame, splintering metal and plastic in all directions. Then with dark eyes he turned to Archer, brandishing the hammer. 'Get the fuck out of here!' Archer's phone began to ring. He fished it out of his pocket.

'It's me,' whispered Goddard.

'This is a *really* bad time...'

'Listen to me. You need to get to the Iceberg Building as soon as you can. You know that...'

'Dad!'

'... that orbiting object the press have been talking about?'

'You mean The Autumn Structure?'

'There's been a development. And... well... you guys need to get down here as soon as you can.'

Archer's eyes landed on Geek's limp body lying on the floor of the tube carriage.

'We're on our way. Please tell me you have a medical facility.'

THE AUTUMN STRUCTURE

London 2060, and thick freezing rain pelted Archer's raincoat as he folded his umbrella and tucked it under his arm. Looking up at the tall, imposing Space Foundation headquarters, the top of the glass shard of the Iceberg Building was swallowed in misty, low-lying cloud. He had no desire to wait inside the huge, airy reception for his colleague in case his father was already waiting for them. Archer didn't feel strong enough to make small talk with the man he had such an angry past with.

No, he would wait for Davey, one of the other members of the Axiom Few, to arrive. Davey was the accountant in his team of freelance techno-graduates. He would be arriving soon, and there would be comfort, and safety, in allies.

Geek however. Well they could only hope for his swift recovery. The Space Foundation only ever called on The Axiom Few when they needed help, and help would be difficult to give when the brains of the team lay in a coma in one of the basement levels of the building he now stood in front of.

Archer moved under an overhanging glass awning at the front of the building and pulled out his phone. On the news website the main headline of the day was the same as it had been for the last week. Growing fear amongst the scientific community of the anomaly the media had been calling "The Autumn Structure". The massive extraterrestrial object had locked itself into orbit approximately 150,000 kilometres above the Earth's surface a week earlier, having appeared out of the Autumn constellation of Pegasus the previous September and tracked on its inbound trajectory for the last six months.

'Archer!' his father shouted to him from the reception door. 'Come and wait inside for God's sake.'

Archer continued scrolling the news item with his thumb; didn't look up. 'Davey won't be long.'

Goddard snuffled a curse that was barely audible but sounded like 'Stupid arsehole,' and hobbled back into the Iceberg Building on his wooden cane. Archer continued to read about the mysterious object that hung in space above him. Their summons was undoubtedly about this. But what could they do, with or without Geek?

The cloud and mist had been burned off by the sun by the time they reached Goddard's office half an hour later, which overlooked the west of the city from a height that revealed London to be a beautifully interspersed medley of the history of industrial construction. Alongside buildings as old as St Paul's Cathedral were towering spires of translucent, angular strength. Buildings seen as beauty to many and a menace to the skyline by others, the only real conclusion can be one of awe. Awe at the way buildings had evolved since they were first engineered.

Archer and Davey sat on the sofa while Goddard took a place at his desk. Once comfortable, the older man said: 'The story about that meteorite that crashed on Dartmoor yesterday is a lie. A fabrication the Space Foundation persuaded the media to release until this crisis is over.'

'What crisis? The Autumn Structure is dormant.'

Goddard was shaking his head, 'Dormant no longer. What actually fell to Earth was a capsule, bound for the Dartmoor Space Foundation Outpost. It didn't impact with the Earth. The capsule decelerated and landed safely in the car park. Does the word "Voidant" mean anything to you?'

Archer and Davey exchanged a glance. The word had a familiar ring to it, but Archer couldn't recall a place where he might have heard it before. Both he and Davey shook their heads. 'What is it?'

'When the capsule landed, a... hatch opened up. I saw it. It opened inwards and this thing came out. A sort of, cubeshaped unit. A box. A metal box glided out. It spoke to us.'

Archer was sitting forward, unaware he had shifted position until he said. 'What did it say?'

'It told us it was a representative of the Voidant. It was almost a Klaatu moment. A "take me to your leader" situation. Who'd have thought that life would imitate art so well...' his voice trailed off and it was a good few seconds before he returned to the moment. 'Anyway, it told us that they had arrived in that ship. The Autumn Structure, as we call it, although the Voidant had another, less pronounceable name. He said his craft is a tool of de- struction, and that if we did not meet his demands, he would use it to destroy the Earth and every living thing on it.'

'What demands?'

'It wants to speak with The Axiom Few.'

The Space Foundation helicopter cut through the sunset on its path across Southern England. Below, the rolling green fields of grass and yellow fields of rape spread out in lush expanse.

Archer consulted his phone. He was in direct contact with the physician at the Iceberg Building who was looking after Geek. They had had to take him to the Space Foundation after he collapsed from using the Capacillant Frame. They couldn't have taken him to a hospital. After what had happened the night be- fore, Geek would be on the hospital watch list. At the Space Foun- dation HQ, he would be safe from the authorities for now.

Rachel, the physician, was posting updates via an encrypted feed. The only update for now, was that there was no update.

Diving into the West Country beyond the city of Exeter the helicopter rose up above the Tors and Beacons of Dartmoor and flew over the barren landscape before descending into a depres- sion, high up on the moor, unseen from any road. The Space Foun- dation Outpost loomed long, low and dark. An ominous scar of a building that had no place nesting in the middle of such beautiful scenery.

Just as they touched down Goddard turn to him. 'I've just received word from the International Space Station that The Autumn Structure has split into two. Prime Minister Armsworth is on his way.'

◆ ◆ ◆

Goddard, Archer and Davey ducked under the spinning blades and ran through the helicopter's fierce draft and high-pitched whine towards a side entrance to the Outpost.

They were escorted down a series of long corridors and within a couple of turns Archer took leave of his sense of direction. If asked to navigate his way out of the place, he would surely be lost in the Outpost for months. They eventually ended up being herded through a small door that looked like the entrance to a broom cupboard, with only the number A117 written above it.

They were led down a set of steps and into a small chamber with concrete walls and a low ceiling with a strip of dimmed halogen lights pointing down to a small wooden table. On top of the table was a small box about half a metre squared. It had no distinguishing features.

'Why the low light?' said Davey.

'Better to see the translucency, when it speaks.'

'What?'

'You'll see.'

And as if on cue, the sides of the box seemed to shimmer and swirl as though made of liquid.

It spoke, matter-of-factly, in a synthesised English voice. 'Archer, Davey. It is a pleasure to finally meet you.'

Inside the box, Archer saw what he could only describe as an organic mesh. Sinews of brown muscle and biomatter stretched to the edges and corners of the inner walls. Pinpoints of light skittered across the muscles, throbbing and collecting in pools across the many surfaces of the Voidant's skin.

'What do you want from us?' he said.

'Where is Geek?'

'Geek... had a better offer.'

A pause. 'Now you are here. I am ready to issue my demands. The demands of the Voidant.'

'Demands?'

'You are no doubt aware that we have the technical capability to destroy this planet. We have the authorisation mandate and tools in orbit now, and we are ready to act on this instruction, if the terms of the first treaty are not met.'

Goddard cleared his throat and spoke, 'What terms? Isn't this something for you to negotiate with our leaders? Not the Axiom Few or us. Our elected leaders speak for us. Why have you come to The Space Foundation?'

'Your leaders cannot agree on anything, and they are most of the problem. If not all of it. Allow me to explain your position. There are a number of ways for a civilisation to evolve and develop. The Voidant have borne witness to many of these methods but they do not all have to be as technological and forceful as the approach taken by humankind. Through barbarism and elitism, the people of Earth have chosen a method of technological and emotional development which is ultimately destructive. You kill each other. You kill yourselves. You abuse your young. You kill the other species you share this planet with. Your collective beliefs are not aligned. These contradictions put you in a terrible position. The irony is that you search for a future that will grant you happiness as a species, but the more you quest, the closer you come to finding the opposite. Humankind has made one too many incorrect choices. You will never be allowed representation on the Council if this is how you choose to progress. We have seen your actions unfold so many times before. We cannot allow you to continue on this course, for the good of the other species we represent, and the harmony of the universe.'

The door to the room opened and a young man walked in. He approached Goddard and whispered in his ear. Goddard nodded, and then whispered to the box, 'You cannot police us.'

'But we can. Others have allowed it and ultimately thanked us for the approach we have taken. You will one day thank us too. It will be millennia from now, but you *will* thank us.'

Goddard said, 'The Prime Minister's helicopter has arrived. He'll be joining us in few minutes. In the meantime we want to know what your terms are. These terms you talked about.'

'The terms are as follows. One. It is a requirement of the council that you revert your conditions to your pre-industrial state. This is a regression of two-hundred and eighty years. We will help you achieve this through the deletion of data from your world servers, and combustion of literature both fictional and non-fictional that has been created since the year 1780. Two. You will surrender to us the top million minds on your planet. We know who they are. We will provide a list for you to inform them. Three...'

'Wait!' said Goddard, 'Wait a minute. How do you plan to take these people? This is ridiculous!'

'Do not worry about the technicalities Goddard. It is not necessary for you to round these individuals up, if that is what you are thinking. We have other, more effective methods. Now if I may be permitted to continue. Our final demand is that the Axiom Few must tell us the location of Brenda.'

At this, Archer and Davey caught each other's eye. There was that name again. They had heard it yesterday when a member of the Precipice Faction had been instructed by Brenda to steal and destroy the Capacillant Frame. But why? What on Earth could the Voidant want with Brenda? Who was she?

Archer fumbled a response. 'We don't know anything about Brenda.'

'But you know the name. I can tell from your voice patterns. The Voidant already know that Brenda is tracking The Axiom Few. Brenda takes great interest in you. If you choose to withhold information about Brenda's location, then it does not matter. Contacting Orbiter. Permission granted to activate demonstration programme...'

There followed a string of garbled noises, a guttural Voidant language that was completely unintelligible. Voidant orders.

The door opened once again and the Prime Minister walked

in, flanked by two plain-clothes security officers. Archer stiffened at his presence. He had never seen Harold Armsworth in the flesh before, only on web broadcasts. He looked much shorter than his televisual representation, but in his sharp well tailored grey suit he seemed imposing nonetheless. Armsworth briefly glimpsed at Archer and Davey, then nodded to Goddard. He didn't seem particularly in awe or fear of the Voidant on the table. Presumably he had been briefed with photographs in advance but his coolness might be attributed to a desire to show strength at a time when it was needed. Or rather, to not show weakness. He opened his mouth and was about to speak when the box spoke first, seemingly not intending to acknowledge that the elected leader of the British Government had just stepped into the chamber. 'Watch your moon.'

The team aboard the ISS looked on in silent awe from a matched velocity as the Autumn Structure, which measured sixteen kilometres from end to end, split into two, some fifty kilometres above them. Each of the two parts now beginning to rotate in opposite directions as they issued a series of thrust bursts and pushed free of Earth's orbit. Accelerating hard as they spun and pitched down and forward they grew smaller and smaller as the moon rose above the hazy curve of the Earth's surface. Then a beam, green in colour and shimmering, was established between the two halves of the Structure, growing in length as the pieces of alien technology drove apart from each other, moonbound. Twisting now, they performed a balletic twirl around each other as they lined up for the lonely crescent, hanging in space above the Earth's dawn terminator. Within minutes the shining green blade, barely visible now, plunged across the moon's distant surface. Cameras aboard the International Space Station recorded the event in extreme zoom as huge plumes of dust billowed powerfully into the sky. And still the tool continued to cut. Between the two beam creators, the celestial knife continued to slice the lunar landscape, tearing what was once such a recognisable sphere into two unrecognisable but equal halves. The force of the ejection of dust, and the power of the seismic event even now began to push the two halves of the moon into separate orbits. Within hours the moon pieces would drift apart enough for the Earth to have twice as many tides in a day, but each only half the strength. With one swift stroke, the Voidant race had doubled the length of time it would take for a human to grow in its mother's womb.'

The box had shown its destructive work by displaying an image taken from one half of the Autumn Structure as it worked to slice the moon like an apple. Now, through translucent surfaces, the Voidant representative spoke once more. 'We will locate Brenda, we will mindsearch the million people once they are aboard our craft. But if we find that you are lying to protect it...'

Silence fell upon the room. The weight of the threat hanging heavy. No one knew how to progress the discussion. The Prime Minister eventually spoke.

'What you have done is a terrible thing. It is an extreme act of war against the human race.'

The Voidant interrupted. 'Items one and two of the treaty are non-negotiable. You have done yourselves no favours by withholding Brenda's location. You have six hours to wipe all data, archival and current, from your world servers and inform the one million individuals that they will be coming with us. Our craft is powerful, well defended, and empty; ready to be filled with your best minds. Human technology is no match for Voidant technology so please do not waste your time with pointless threats and even more pointless action. Your cards have been dealt.'

The helicopter flew lower and faster over the fields and towns on the way back to the roof of the Iceberg Building. Archer used his phone to contact Rachel.

'Rachel, you need to wake Geek up. He needs to come out of his coma *right now*.'

A sigh from the other end of the line. 'I can't sanction that.'

'But there are methods, aren't there? Methods to wake him.'

'Archer...'

'Tell me...'

A long pause on the line. The helicopter skirted round the environs of Heathrow Base and banked north towards the looming city. Urban lights twinkled in the evening haze. 'Yes. We can perform Deep Brain Stimulation. Plant electrodes to bring him back. But there's absolutely no betting that he'll recover in the way that you need him to. You may end up killing him.'

'We may be killing him if we don't do this. Killing us all. Please Rachel. We have no choice. The PM has authorised it. I know it's not the best thing to do. But the alternative is far, far worse.'

Archer and Davey were sitting at Geek's bedside when his eyes fluttered open at just after two o'clock in the morning. He smiled when he saw his colleagues in the room. But then his smiling eyes darkened. 'I have a thousand things I need to tell you.'

Archer rested a hand on his arm. 'Steady on.'

Geek shook his head slowly, painfully. His speech slurred. 'No, we really need to talk. The Frame. When... when I was in the Capacillant Frame I saw things. Things you need to know about.'

'Geek, please go easy.'

'I understand what Brenda is. We need to find it. I know where to locate the Brenda device. Also, also I have seen. There is a fourth member. A fourth member of the Axiom Few. I know who he is.'

Archer shared a glance with Davey, and looked up to Rachel, but she had her back to the room.

'Geek, we've made first contact with the Voidant. They arrived in that thing we called The Autumn Structure. They want to take a million of the best minds on the planet. You're one of them.'

Geek smiled knowingly, slowly nodding. 'A harvest. An Autumn harvest. Whoever named that thing, they probably knew more than they were letting on.'

'They want us to regress and unlearn our technology to a pre-industrial era. They want us to...'

'It's ok Archer. I know what they want. I've seen it. The Capacillant Frame did everything I thought it would.'

Davey leaned forward. 'Why do the Voidant want Brenda?'

The electronics in the room died. Fans whirred down to nothing and beeping ceased. Geek tried to sit up. 'It's happening.'

'Yes.'

Geek tried to swallow through a clicking dry throat. 'Water.'

He drunk from the cup Archer offered to his lips. 'Listen to me. Both of you.' Geek spoke quietly through gritted teeth. 'They mustn't find Brenda. They *mustn't!* It will mark the beginning of the end of humanity.'

Geek started to become invisible. Davey said, 'They're taking him.'

Geek spoke quickly, with more strain in his voice. 'Brenda is... our protector. It is imperative that it is not disconnected. Brenda knows how to stop the Voidant War and it must be allowed to continue its work. It tries to protect itself, but it cannot do it all by itself. It needs help from humans. From *us*. Brenda's location is secret, but I know how to get to it.'

Davey kicked back his chair. Standing, he held fast onto Geek's arm. But how do you stop someone from vanishing into thin air. Though Geek was fading, his voice remained clear. 'You must understand. The Capacillant Frame helped me to see. Everything happens at once in the multiverse. There is someone who can help you.'

'Who? Tell me.'

'He also used it. He also knows. He was a... dribbling clown. Now I understand... why it was so easy for us to get to him. Brenda must have engine.... The database... He must have infiltrated the Faction to gain access to... the Frame. You *must* find him.'

And with that, Geek disappeared into thin air.

THE AXIOM NASCENCY

Brighton 2053, and a turbulent dark winter sea threw up icy spray across the tide defence walls as Archer cut away from the coast road on foot and hurried home through the back lanes. He arrived home to the familiar sight of his father, Goddard, sitting in an armchair in the living room, staring into the open fire which roared in the fireplace, a large tumbler of whisky in hand. Rain incessantly rolled at the windows.

Archer sat down on the sofa. 'Dad, it was a really productive day at the components fair. I've seen some really cool gadgetry and it's given me some ideas for...'

'Listen, do you mind if we catch up in the morning?'

Archer looked to the rain-spattered window, wishing he was back on the other side of it, and then at the pathetic figure that sat opposite him. Today, it seemed, was no different to the rest. 'I thought you might be interested in what I'm doing.' He stood up and made for the door. 'See you in the morning.'

Behind him came a sigh from the older man. 'I'm sorry, I didn't mean... Why don't you come and sit down.'

'Dad! Why don't *you* snap out of your angry fucking stupor?'

Goddard twisted in his chair to look his son in the eye. 'Don't you dare speak to me like that!'

'Nobody else is going to. Go on. Tell me the answer. When are you going to put *me* out of *your* misery?'

Goddard was rubbing his temples in a manner that said, "not again". 'Please Archer...'

Archer strode towards the windows and faced his father head on. He knew he was acting like the embodiment of a snowball now. His anger on a downward slope, gathering pace and momentum. Unstoppable and growing in size. 'It's been twenty years. I'm twenty now. Nothing we can do will bring her back but you insist on holding this… this candle like it's going to reverse things.'

'Archer, please. It's just that,' Goddard stood up, uneasy on his feet. His whisky breath stinking into Archer's face. 'It's just that…'

'Let me finish that sentence for you. It's just that you wish she'd never gotten pregnant with me. You would rather she was here, than me.'

'You…' Goddard swiped a drunken hand at Archer and his lazy fist connected with his son's cheek, knocking him sideways just enough for him to have to work hard to keep from falling back against a free-standing lamp. 'You *arsehole* Archer! You absolute arsehole. You have everything to be grateful for. *Everything.*'

'Don't you dare fucking hit me! I'll call the fucking police on you.'

Goddard, unsteady on his feet, took one step forward and pointed a finger into Archer's face, jabbing a nail into his son's right cheek and drawing blood. 'I brought you into this world and I can bloody well take you out of it. You ungrateful little shit.'

Archer delivered a sharp downward kick to his father's shin. His boot connected with a snap of bone and at that instant Archer knew he had gone too far. His father gave a guttural, phlegmy roar of pain and collapsed to the floor, his head connected with the arm of the chair he had just gotten up from. Did Archer hear something snap? Wood or bone? Without waiting a moment longer, he ran out into the soaking night.

Dark ships with tiny twinkling lights littered the English Channel. Even through the rain Archer could see those beacons of transport and industry cruising through the ill-lit waterway.

From where he stood at the end of Brighton's now derelict Palace Pier, with the turbulent winter sea churning beneath him and the freezing horizontal rain stinging his cheeks, not a soul could be seen, but on the shore the thrumming of nightclubs and the yelling of partygoers was carried to him on the wind. That other people were having more fun only angered him more. That they could enjoy their young lives without a weight of guilt hanging about their neck only served to reinforce his current thinking.

And like a free runner, he vaulted over the railing, effortless and almost unthinking. As he plummeted past the wooden deck of the pier, he caught the briefest sight of a figure, silhouetted in the door of the old amusement arcade.

His last thought before the icy cold swept the breath from his body was that someone had seen him jump.

'I want to ask you some questions.'

'Who are you?' Why can't I see you?'

'I am in another room, but my voice is coming from the speaker built into the box on the table in front of you.'

'Why am I here?'

'You jumped from the end of Palace Pier into the sea two nights ago. You were rescued, revived in hospital, and brought here.'

'You haven't answered my question. Who are you?'

'For now, you can call me Gerald.'

'For now? What about later?'

'We shall cross that bridge when we get there. Tell me. What prompted you to take your own life?'

'Am I dead?'

'I will repeat the question. What prompted..?'

'I heard the question. I... I was angry.'

'About what?'

'My father. He's such... I hate him. I hate him because he hates me and it's not my fault.'

'What is not your fault?'

'Why won't you let me speak to you face to face?'

'All in good time. You were saying about your father?'

Archer rubbed his eyes, as though such an act would aid clarity of thought. 'He blames me for my Mum's death. She lost... she lost a lot of blood when she was giving birth to me. She had a rare blood group and there wasn't enough of it in the hospital store. She lost too much and she lost consciousness and they couldn't revive her. Dad. He looks at me and sees what I did to her. Unintentionally. I didn't *ask* to be born but he doesn't see it that way. So I decided. I thought I would put myself out of his misery.'

'Are you aware that it is illegal to take your own life?'

'I don't care,' said Archer, struggling to comprehend the audacity of the question. 'If I'd succeeded then I would have been happy to stand trial. My body, however, is not the responsibility of the state.'

'It is the state's responsibility to protect you from yourself.'

'Bullshit. My life is my own.'

'Think of the authorities that were mobilised to rescue you from the sea. The taxpayers would prefer their hard-earned money to be spent on sending the coastguard to rescue people who...'

'Who *want* to be rescued! You've underlined my point. I didn't *want* to be rescued. The coastguard could have saved their time and resources.'

'Just a moment.'

'Who are you people?'

'Just a moment.'

'Why won't you let me g...'

'Rec... just a moment.'

Footsteps out in the corridor. Running. They stopped just the other side of the door to the room and then a bolt was thrown. The door flew open and a young man strode in. Skinny, in a white short-sleeved t-shirt with the word GEEK written on it. He moved over to the box, lifted his leg, and booted it with one swift kick. 'Fucking thing!'

Archer laughed. 'What?'

'I knew it wasn't ready. Cheap bloody RAM.'

'Who are you?'

'The young man seemed to snap out of some sort of red trance, noticed Archer, and then extended his hand. 'Sorry, I'm Nathaniel.'

Archer shook it. 'Archer. Where am I?'

Nathaniel sighed. 'Look, I'm sorry about the interrogation. We were toying with whether to use it, but it's clearly not ready for a proper... y'know. Frankly I'm amazed they let me use it on an actual suic...' He checked himself, and fell silent.

'What was that you were saying about the cheap RAM?' said Archer.

'What? Oh. Don't worry. The College said I could practice using the Communi-K on a real case. You know, a real suicide case.'

'Communique?'

Geek pointed at the box. 'This thing. It's spelled with a K. Like, you know... Communi-K. Something I knocked together but I'm working on the name.'

'A Turing device?'

'Yeah I guess so. I'm pretty far down with the mechanics of the dialogue, but then it keeps hanging and I keep upgrading the hardware. But it still hangs. If it has to hold more than a set number of potential concepts in memory then it just conks out. Like I said, cheap RAM. Wish I could afford Techipre RAM, but that stuff's quality and my budget doesn't stretch that far.'

Archer stood up. 'Do you know what? I might be able to help you with that.'

Geek cocked his head, almost like a dog listening. 'Really?'

'Yeah, I was at their component fair the other day.'

'The component fair? But that was two days ago... well it would have been the day you jumped, right?'

'Yeah, and I love that you don't seem to give a toss about that.'

Geek shrugged. 'You were saying about the Techipre RAM?'

'I know a guy there. He's the account manager for the organisation my father works for. I can get good deals through him, due to the volume of business he gets from my Dad.'

'Is this the same Dad you can't stand the sight of?'

Archer nodded. 'He works for the Space Foundation. He's pretty high up, and very successful. But he lives in austerity and comes home every night to nurse a bottle of whisky and he blames me for Mum. She died while I was being born. And he seems to think I had a hand in it. Like I had some sort of power to exit differently when I was brought kicking and screaming into the world.'

Geek seemed aloof at these facts. 'So you're a techie?'

'In a past life. I'd build stuff. Take stuff apart. I made a dongle once that crashed the Tesco Network for six hours.'

Geek laughed. 'That's pretty good.'

Archer pointed to the Communi-K. 'Not as good as this thing. This is cutting edge stuff, even if it does have a rubbish name.'

'Yeah, well I dabble in components too. My Dad was jailed for corporate fraud. After that I vowed never to join the big league. I prefer to work on my own.'

'You're working here.'

'Well spotted! I have an arrangement. Listen, do you have a bed to sleep in tonight?'

'Are you hitting on me?'

'No, not like that. I have a friend I should introduce you to. Davey. He's into this stuff too. Tech stuff. But he works at the homeless shelter in Charing Cross. He can probably help you.' He leaned closer and whispered, 'I can get you rubberstamped out of here provided you don't try to top yourself again.'

'I'm grateful. I really am. By the way... What the hell is this place?'

Archer and Geek exited the King's College South Bank campus and walked north across Waterloo Bridge.

'I have an arrangement with them,' said Geek. 'I help them with research and they put me up in the halls of residence and feed me. They did a deal with the Sussex authorities to do some research and development into the psychology of suicide cases. You know, the Beachy Head alumni.'

'I didn't fancy Beachy Head. Too far from home. In my red mist, I only made it as far as Palace Pier.'

'Thankfully you were still in Sussex. Which meant that the

responsibility for your rehabilitation fell into the hands of the college. They wanted me to test out the Communi-K on you, but I knew it wasn't ready. I'd been begging for more money to get better parts but, you know how these things work.'

The London skyline to the east of the bridge was as striking as ever. The curves of St Paul's and the Gherkin set against the straight lines of the Docklands looming in the distance. Cranes turning and building ever more ambitious skyscrapers in the square mile. Beacons of commerce towering over the preserved antiquities of old banks, libraries and courthouses. And still the Thames flowed through them.

'Why would anyone want to use an artificial intelligence device on a suicide case?'

'It's a cost-cutting exercise. Staff reductions across the board in the rehabilitation sector mean that it's better for the budget if computers can do some of this stuff. From an R&D point of view, well you're a lost cause. What more do we have to lose? Maybe you can be rehabilitated. Maybe you can't.'

'That's a hard line.'

'Look, you would have regretted it in the morning. That tells me there's something worth saving. AI can look at the facts objectively. Deal with your case more intelligently than a human can.'

Archer let this thought sink in. Had society really come to this? The disposability of people's feelings in the face of budget cuts and accountability? He was about to challenge this when Geek added. 'If you don't like it we can toss you back in the sea. Or there's a perfectly good river right underneath us.'

Geek's friend David Hallam met them on the wide steps on the north side of Trafalgar Square. The winter sun did little to banish the iciness from the air but the day was beautifully cloudless. The church of St Martin in the Fields chimed two o'clock above the sound of afternoon cars.

Seemingly no older than Geek, David had long, straggly blond hair that looked like it had been recently braided. He was tall, tanned and healthy looking, despite wearing torn jeans and a grey fleece that looked like it had seen better days.

The three of them sat on the cold steps drinking coffee from polystyrene cups brought by David on a tray from the homeless shelter. Archer found it strange that they sipped and blew on hot coffee in silence for a good minute, seemingly sharing a quiet moment that under any other circumstances could have been awkward. For a small, strange moment Archer felt that the three of them had known each other for years.

To the south, beyond the glittering lights in the Norwegian Christmas tree that adorned the square every year, Big Ben stood high above Parliament Square at the other end of Whitehall. As he looked at the famous clock tower, Archer began to realise that there was nothing for him in Brighton anymore. London was where he needed to be, where he would make his second stand, whether he deserved such a chance or not.

David eventually leaned forward and looked past Geek at Archer. 'I gather you need a bed for the night?'

Archer nodded. 'Can you help?'

David smiled. 'Of course. You'll be fine. But don't be homeless for long mate. It's no good for anybody. In fact, I'm on the night watch tonight. If you want to come on my rounds, you can meet some other homeless folks, and see exactly why you don't want to go down that road.'

Geek finished his coffee, swallowed hard and said to his friend, 'Are you going after that kid again? The kid that told us about...'

David was nodding, staring at Geek. 'I want to find him.'

Archer said, 'What kid?'

David looked up at Nelson's Column for a moment and said, 'Just this weird kid. Weird, ha! That's a term they don't let me use in the shelter.'

'What weird kid?'

Looking uncomfortable now, David glanced hard at Geek in a look that said, "Why did you open up this subject" but he spoke nonetheless. 'Three nights ago this teenager walks into the shelter. I'd seen him before; he's been homeless for about two months. Says he saw someone jump into the sea in Brighton. Off Palace Pier'

Archer's heart jumped. 'Was he talking about me?'

David nodded. 'Said you could still be saved if the coastguard was quick enough.'

'But how would he know?'

Geek shrugged, 'That's the weird thing. This kid told Davey to contact me at the College and get me to contact the Sussex authorities, like he *knew* about the College's arrangement.'

Archer thought for a moment about the moment that he jumped. They were mostly cold thoughts, and he could remember the way his bones felt like they had been shoved into a deep freeze. Cold to the core.

'Someone was there when I jumped. I saw a person standing in the doorway to the amusement arcade at the end of the pier. I saw, but how would he have gotten to London quick enough to inform you *and* be convinced it wasn't too late to save me? It's not possible to survive in cold water for that long.'

'It's like he teleported or something,' said Geek.

'Or time-travelled,' added David.

Archer laughed. 'Except we all know that time travel is theoretically impossible. Maybe he phoned someone. It couldn't have been the same person.'

David was looking at Geek, grinning. He was sharing a joke with his friend. Geek however was watching a group of tourists and seemed to be trying to ignore his friend. Eventually, after an awkward silence, he shot a glance at David. It was a "why did you have to bring this up" type look.

This made Archer wonder why they both were keen to reveal so much and yet so little to him?

Geek eventually said. 'This is a digression but, I've been working on something. Something that might do it.'

'Do what?'

Geek continued. 'I call it the Epoch Tunnel.'

Realising they were still on the subject of time-travel, Archer leaped to his feet, standing in front of Geek. 'You're shitting me! Does it work?'

Geek raised his hands, casting his eyes about him, 'Sit down, please.'

Archer did, taking a mouthful of coffee. Geek took a deep breath. 'I sent a monkey seventy-eight minutes into the future.'

It was such a ridiculous statement that Archer sprayed his coffee a full six feet from all the laughing. His laughter turned into an uncontrollable cough.

Geek looked at David in a "see?" type gesture.

Archer coughing eventually eased. 'Seriously? Seventy-eight minutes? What happened to it?'

Geek shrugged, 'It disappeared and reappeared seventy eight minutes later.'

'Was it okay?'

Geek nodded. 'Yeah it was fine. It took me a while to calibrate the latitudinal anchor. Before I did that, a subject that moved forward in time didn't also move forward in space. It leaped over the time gap, but not the space gap.'

'What Geek means,' added David, 'is that the first monkey he sent through the tunnel reappeared seventy-eight minutes later, somewhere in space, due to the Earth's motion around the sun. But he's fixed that now.'

Archer couldn't help but shake his head. 'That's incredible! Have you tried it on a h..?'

David interrupted, whispering. 'Shh! Shit! It *is* him!' Archer and Geek both turned to look at David.

'What are you on about?' said Geek.

'Don't look now, but I've just spotted him.'

'You mean the kid? Where?'

'The steps of the National Gallery, behind us. On the left side. Black trousers, green fleece, dark hair, with a rucksack. He's watching us.'

Archer whispered, 'How long has he been there?'

'I've no idea. But the fact he's watching us at all is scaring the hell out of me.'

Archer stood up, rubbed his hands, saw the kid from the corner of his eye. 'Let's go and have a chat shall we?'

Geek looked up at him. 'Are you sure you want to hear what he might have to say, even if you could get it out of him?'

'What's *that* supposed to mean?' And then Archer was up the wide steps that spanned the centre of the square, bounding up two at a time. At six foot three in height, his legs were long and they carried him at great speed towards the young man who had been watching them. But the kid had already seen Archer moving towards him and had jumped the last three steps to the main concourse on the square. Now he was breaking into a run, westwards, in the direction of Pall Mall. Archer picked up speed, giving chase, not caring whether Geek and David were following behind.

Cutting through a small crowd of tourists who were waiting for a sightseeing bus outside the Sainsbury Wing of the Gallery, the kid with the rucksack pushed on a further hundred metres towards the bottom of Haymarket, jumping out into traffic and risking life and limb to get to the opposite corner by New Zealand House, and on he ran, seemingly with unlimited energy. But in his past life Archer had been a regular runner along the promenade by the sea, an interest that had followed on from winning the annual athletic championships at school. Those morning runs were now paying off as he gained ever so slightly on the escaping kid.

But then the traffic lights hindered his chase, and he was forced to wait as a string of buses and coaches seared through the lights and round the corner.

Geek and David caught up with him in the time it took for the traffic to clear, and David said, 'I can still see him. He's turned right onto Lower Regent Street.'

Then a gap in the traffic appeared and Archer leapt back into a full pelt, leaving the other two in his wake.

Round the corner into Lower Regent Street now, just in time to see the kid with the rucksack disappear left into Charles II Street, and Archer carelessly dived out into the road to sprint across it diagonally, weaving through stationary taxis caught in a jam that led all the way up to Piccadilly Circus. He waved behind him, pointing southwest, indicating for the others to run straight along Pall Mall, which would serve as a good way of preventing their prey from cutting south toward the Mall. The problem would arise if the kid ran north, as the roads fanned out into an ancient maze, which would undoubtedly render him almost impossible to find.

On Charles II Street now, and Archer was gaining once again on the kid, who, as he was now in the back streets, did not have the luxury of a traffic jam to facilitate a larger gap between him and his advancing predator, but still he ran, through the gate that led into the green tree-lined space in the centre of St James's Square.

He ran along the central path and around the statue of William III, swerving around a walker here and there, before joining another path that led to the opposite gate. Soon he would be on King Street, home of Christie's auctioneer.

But Archer was now a mere thirty metres behind him; as he had closed the gap by more than half since they departed Trafalgar Square. Unless this kid had something up his sleeve, this chase would be over soon, and to Archer's advantage.

Archer now wondered if there was a way he could force the kid to turn south, into the clutches of Geek and David.

But it was something he couldn't rely on.

On King Street now, dashing along the south pavement, and the kid's stamina was ebbing, enabling Archer, whose breathing had barely become laboured, to close the gap to ten metres. Then an even better thing happened.

South into Angel Court, a tiny alleyway that led between King Street and Pall Mall. With a bit of luck, Geek and David would arrive at the other end and be able to trap the kid. But as Archer rounded the corner into the lonely alleyway he saw that the other two had not arrived.

But the kid had stopped and was kneeling down by the wall, digging around in his rucksack. He was saying something; talking to himself in a low voice. 'Task forty-seven complete. Few assembled.'

Archer stopped a few feet away. 'Why were you watching us?'

The kid didn't answer, or even look up. He had retrieved a small black plastic box measuring about twenty centimetres cubed, with two handholds protruding from each side. An amber light was flashing next to one of the handholds. 'Brenda, I'm ready to transfer to the next branch.'

Archer spoke again. 'Hey, I'm talking to you. Who are you speaking to?'

'Priming the Threader now.'

'Did you watch me jump? Tell me! Were you there? On the pier?'

The kid finally looked up. He seemed impatient with his device, as though he was willing it to reach some sort of readystate, but it wasn't happening quickly enough. 'Don't speak to me.'

Archer took a step forward, and the kid raised his hand, 'I said, please keep away from me.'

'No! Answer my questions. What are you doing?'

Standing up slowly now, picking up the device with one hand, holding the rucksack with the other. 'Please! Stay back!'

In a swift move Archer leaned forward and grabbed the rucksack. This was a development that shocked the kid as his jaw dropped open in an expression of surprise and terror. 'No!'

And the kid pulled, but his little finger was trapped between two straps and a clasp. Archer yanked abruptly and heard a feint pop as the kid's finger slipped out of its joint. The look of surprise on the kid's face turned swiftly to a grimace of pain as he realised what Archer had just done to him. But before the moment had a chance to develop, the amber light on the small box in his other hand turned green and he immediately vanished into thin air, leaving Archer holding the rucksack, with a little bloodied finger wedged between two of the straps.

Archer let out a yelp that sounded like it had come from someone else, and pulled the finger away from the rucksack, throwing it down in disgust, where it hit the floor, rolled two feet, and disappeared into a pile of leaves.

Loud running footsteps from the south end of the alleyway.

Geek and David appeared there, silhouetted by the daylight behind them but soon coming properly into view as they ran quickly to meet Archer.

'Where is he?'

'He disappeared.'

'Where?'

'No, I mean he actually vanished… into nothing.'

'You've got his bag.'

'I took it off him. He had a box with him. He used it to disappear.'

Geek took the rucksack from Archer and opened it up. He removed a small pair of goggles with data connectors on one side, and a ragged scrapbook. 'That's all that's here. I recognise this. This book.'

Geek fanned the pages. 'This is my book. I have one of these back at the college. But it's not as full as this one. I've only filled the first page of mine but…'

Archer put out his hand 'Let's see.'

Geek handed it to him. 'I don't get it.'

Looking at the first page, Archer saw the diagrams of a recognisable device, and a heading that read "Communi-K".

'That's all I'd filled in on mine,' added Geek. 'The first page.' Geek and David leaned in to look as Archer flipped to the next page, which described a Light Distortion Jacket.

David said, 'That's your handwriting Geek.'

'Yes, but I never wrote this. I didn't write this. I've been thinking about some sort of invisibility jacket but…'

The next page showed a diagram of the goggles that lay on the floor. The title read "Reflection Goggles".

The page after that showed a headset device called a ComArc, drawn in the same hand and with annotation in Geek's alleged handwriting.

The next page. Archer recognised the box that the kid had been holding the moment he vanished.

At the top were three names, the first two crossed out.

Epoch Bridge. Crossed out.

Epoch Tunnel. Crossed out.

Epoch Threader. Archer pointed at this. 'He had this in his hand. He said he was priming the Threader.'

'Has this guy stolen my inventions?'

'Inventions you haven't made yet,' said David.

The next page showed a diagram of a device called the Capacillant Frame. 'What the hell is a Capacillant Frame?'

The next page. A Jolian Trenchvice, then a DataSurface Scope, a Spinequake Register, a Cassandra Thoughtwave, an Extinction Frequency, a Paradox Interdictor. On and on the pages went, full of ideas and inventions that would one day be Geek's, as all the notes were written in his hand.

Geek stepped away from the others, pacing, scratching his head. 'Who the hell was that guy?'

Archer looked up from the book. 'He didn't say.'

David said, 'We need to make some of this stuff. This book is really helpful. We need to start working on this stuff. Geek? What do you think?'

Geek stopped pacing and looked at Archer. 'You said you have a contact at Techipre that can get us cheap, good quality components?'

'I do,' said Archer, feeling a sense of momentum, of growing energy. Of a future of promise, on the brink of some serious science. Now *that* was something to live for!

David said. 'Then all we need is somewhere to work.'

Geek was nodding, his eyes darting left to right. Thinking. Thinking. 'Don't worry about that. I know somewhere we can go. I've had my eye on a place. It's a disused shack...'

ACKNOWLEDGEMENTS

I would like to thank the following people for their contributions either directly or indirectly to this collection of stories. Firstly to Ian Redman, editor of Jupiter SF magazine, for seeing the potential in The Ceres Configuration and me back in 2004 and placing the story within his pages, as well as two further stories in the series, The Darken Loop and The Voidant Lance. He very nearly accepted The Techipre Filament, but by then he rightly thought that the Axiom Few concept was growing too big to be supported by individual short stories. For the contribution of certain ideas that made that first story flow much better than my original drafts, I would like to thank my dad, Mike, who also produced the superb cover illustration. I would also like to thank the various online reviewers, namely Adrian Fry, Annieworld, Sam Tomaino of SFRevu and Rich Horton of SFSite, whose praise acted as great encouragement to continue writing Axiom Few stories. It was their excellent feedback for The Darken Loop and The Voidant Lance which prompted me to explore the deeper implications of the seeds I'd planted in those early stories. Rod MacDonald I would especially like to thank for adding his wonderful introduction to this edition and for championing the Jupiter SF stories in his SFCrowsnest reviews. I would like to thank my mum, Marilyn, who doesn't always get the science but is never short of encouragement and inspiration. Finally, to my wonderful wife Alison, who has to put up with my daydreaming on a daily basis, and is always so supportive.

Errors and inconsistencies across the stories I would like to say are symptomatic of writing an evolving canon over a number of years. Of course, the truth of the matter is that in our endlessly branching multiverse, there are no errors, just versions of reality where things turn out differently...

Huw Langridge
September 2010

ABOUT THE AUTHOR

Huw Langridge

Thanks to his English teacher at Holland Park School, Huw Langridge realised that writing (and reading) was actually pretty enjoyable, but it wasn't until a few things happened during the 1990s that he realised that he could be inspired into bringing out his own literary voice.

Whilst lying on his back in the middle of a starry night with a bunch of friends on a summer beach holiday in Selsey Bill, staring into space while a CD player filled their heads with the epic 46-minute ambient track "Waiting for Cousteau" by Jean-Michel Jarre, Huw was filled with the vertiginous sensation that he could actually by lying on the bottom of the Earth, looking down at the universe, and it was only a little bit of gravity that was holding him in place.

A few years later, his father spent half of a meal in a London restaurant raving about a book he'd been reading about a cylindrical spaceship that was 40 kilometres wide. Huw started reading Arthur C Clarke's Rendezvous with Rama himself and has since been smitten with hard sci-fi.

This was compounded by a cinema visit to have his mind expanded by the film Contact, which made him want to write his own kind of widescreen science fiction.

He grew up in London and, during his years working as a global IT troubleshooter for an oil exploration company, Huw travelled to a number of places that enabled him to find inspiration and tone for his stories. More recently he has travelled the world working on an operations team delivering high-calibre investment conferences.

In July 2003 Huw attended an Arvon Foundation novel-writing course at the residential retreat at Lumb Bank in Yorkshire. The course was tutored by Martyn Bedford ("The Houdini Girl" and "Acts of Revision") and Phil Whitaker ("Triangulation" and "The Face"). The guest author was Louise Welsh ("The Cutting Room"). Also in attendance was Ian Marchant ("Parallel Lines"). Huw has cooked for all of them, and is glad they survived the ordeal.

Huw's first short story publication was the science fiction piece "The Ceres Configuration", published in Issue 4 of Jupiter SF Magazine, released in April 2004. The story was described by Adrian Fry of Whispers of Wickedness as "A good old fashioned (yet high-tech) tale of approaching apocalypse, [which] served to remind me just what unpretentious science fiction can do when written by someone who clearly relishes every word."

In Autumn 2004 he produced an eNovel called Spireclaw.

Huw released his first print novel Schaefer's Integrity in December 2008 and is available at all major online booksellers. Further published short works have appeared in The Ranfurly Review, Reflection's Edge, Jupiter SF, 365tomorrows and Supernatural Tales.

His short story "Last Train to Tassenmere" received an Honorable Mention in Ellen Datlow's Year's Best Horror 2009.

In September 2010 he released his short story collection The Axiom Few, featuring three previously published stories and five stories new to the collection. His Axiom Few stories have received praise from a number of online SF review websites, such as SF Signal, SF Site and SF Crowsnest.

After his eNovel "Spireclaw" received praise online, Huw decided to release a non-profit print version which came out in September 2011.

Further short story collections include a set of ghost stories entitled "The Train Set" and a book of science fiction shorts called "A Comet of Ideas Looking for a Planet", both available on Kindle.

In 2020 he published his latest novel The Tolworth Beacon.

Huw gets his inspiration from music, travel and the seasons. He lives by the sea in North Wales with his wife and two children.

Printed in Great Britain
by Amazon

17925204R10082